THE SHADOW OF MUSSOLINI

THE SHADOW OF MUSSOLINI

BY

MRS. WILFRID WARD

AUTHOR OF
" THE JOB SECRETARY," " ONE POOR SCRUPLE "
"OUT OF DUE TIME," " HORACE BLAKE "
ETC., ETC.

WILDSIDE PRESS

PRINTED IN GREAT BRITAIN BY J. AND J. GRAY, EDINBURGH

CONTENTS

BOOK I

5

CONTENTS

AUTHOR'S NOTE

A ROMANCE is essentially an irresponsible thing. Its characters are not of the real world. They are drawings of the author's thoughts for the diversion of the reader. If here or there a famous name is introduced, or a great man is made to move in this imaginary world, it is because we all live under the shadow of great men, and their influence on the purely imaginary characters of a novel will be similar to that which they would exercise on real men and women. There are no drawings from life in this book; except of course that of the Duce, whose shadow is cast over the whole world of our time. But if none of the other characters have lived in the real world, they may yet help us to a closer view of that one who is at least very actively alive.

BOOK I

CHAPTER I

"YOUTH! SPRINGTIME! BEAUTY!"

A CHURCH is often described as perched on a height to convey the precarious effect that can have such a charm ; but this church was not perched on the mountain-top, but embedded like a fossil in its higher rocks. The shrine was narrow, dark and high. It may have been accurately orientated, but if that were so the brilliance of the very early morning was kept off it by the shoulder of the peak. In the same shadow was the bleak narrow presbytery, of which the door was already open. A holdall, a strapped Japanese basket and a lady's umbrella were laid on the doorstep. From the wide steep cobbled path that led to the church a narrow one diverged to the presbytery. The two buildings were on a small shelf of the mountain, above which an impossible path rose and disappeared in the crags.

The interior of the presbytery was bare and dull, but by the sad inhabitant about to leave it it was beloved. She was a tall young woman, not valued merely for her looks, for, owing to the peculiar circumstances of her life, her other gifts had been considered to be more remarkable than the beauty of her face. Hers was not the slow, ruminating, dull, large-eyed type that is too often represented as typically Italian, nor did she, like some of her countrywomen, give the impression of being angry or down-trodden. There was the light of a cultivated intelligence in the dark eyes, and the head had the pose of a conscious liberty. Anybody who had lived long in Florence might have guessed that she was a citizen of the town beloved by Dante.

She stood by the kitchen table, a tall figure that had simple outlines from the straight folds of the widow's veil on the hat to the long lines of the cloak that hung from her shoulders. She made a last close scrutiny of the room, not only because she loved it, but because she was determined to make it impossible for the newcomers to complain. She had herself worked hard to help the old servant, once her nurse, who had gone home yesterday, to leave it in order. There was something of the grand manner, the large Italian gesture that was utterly unconscious as she looked up at the old Crucifix blackened by centuries of wood smoke, crossed herself and went out of the house. There she stood for a moment considering her mean impedimenta. The climb of a mile or more down that stony cobbled path with such a load was a serious proposition. She counted on her fingers and on each finger she mentioned the name of a young man—yes there were seven or eight or ten any one of whom would have carried that luggage and been proud to do it at one time, who would not lift a little finger to help her now. With a shrug of her shoulders she turned to the church, taking her load with her. The light in the red sanctuary lamp was burning low when she entered. It was a place of popular pilgrimage, but it was famous chiefly for the fourteen chapels which were scattered on the pathway rising from the Lake of Como, with their terra-cotta, life-sized representations of scenes in the life of Christ. The church itself was obviously many centuries older than the chapels ; but it was the latter that attracted all sorts and conditions of foreign visitors. It is, indeed, a wonderful walk, or rather a wonderful climb, from the little pier at Campo, as at every chapel there is revealed a new view of the far-stretching Lake of Como and the mountains beyond. Each chapel as it is reached affords a new resting-place after a footsore struggle up the cobbled pathway. Occasionally there is a green grass terrace for which the weary are very grateful. Inside the church there is the strongest contrast with the baroque chapels that lead up to it and their somewhat melodramatic groups of figures. All within is grey and stern, even the old quaint pictures and samplers representing in the strangest needlework miraculous cures of illness and equally miraculous rescues from drowning in the waters of the exquisite but treacherous Lake of Como. The place was often crowded to suffocation when pilgrimages came from a distance, from Milan and even further. But no one lived on the rocky ledge of the mountain except the priest in charge, and in the case of the last priest his sister also.

The priest's sister moved about the church now rapidly—not in any mouse-like way—with swift

13

movements unconsciously tragic. She replenished the lamp with oil, she relit the votive candles round the statue of the Madonna. She put out the beautiful old vestments on the age-blackened oak table in the sacristy. Then she paused. But it was not the extraordinary magnificence of the scene below her, the immense extension of lake and mountains that kept her for a moment at the window; it was the sound of young voices, men's voices singing snatches of a song that was lost and came again quite distinctly as they followed the windings of the cobbled path: " *Giovinezza* . . . *Primavera* . . . *Bellezza* "—words banal enough in themselves; but what a ring in the voices—the trumpet note too was in it. Sons of the morning these young men, singing or calling with an austere joy. She knew them; they were the young men whose names she had counted on her fingers. They emerged presently on a little green terrace between two of the chapels following a black figure in a cassock. They were the voluntary escort of the new priest. They were carrying his luggage, much larger and heavier than her own, up the heights.

They passed the church and deposited the priest's luggage inside the presbytery. The watcher in the church could see them come out and the priest with them, evidently thanking them with some cheery jest. To this they responded with the famous Fascist salute, the salute of old Rome, and in a moment the noble-faced youths disappeared, rapidly descending the cobbled pathway. The priest stood watching them. The old face had caught the joyous

light lit by the noble aspirations in young hearts.
He saw in these lovers of their country the glory
that was new and yet old.

> " Tutti assorti nel nuovo destino
> Certi in cor del antica virtu."

It was now safe to come out of the church and
begin going down the mountain. A moment later,
out of sight at one corner of the green terrace, stood
the tall figure in her long grey cloak surrounded by her
mean-looking luggage. They had known quite well,
those sons of the morning, that no one would lift
a finger to help her. It was nearly six o'clock and
the boat for Como left at seven. She was feeling quite
calm now, she even looked lovingly at the great
glories of that indescribable vast extent beneath.
Would she be able to see it in her mind wherever she
might be in a drab and sordid world ? Then she rose,
took the two pieces of luggage well balanced, and
with a good swing started along the terrace. How it
was done she hardly knew. She thought her angel
guardian had given her a helping hand, but she was
at the little pier in time. She would have been easily
first on the boat, but looking back she saw coming
down the road the same young men who had escorted
the priest, every one of them known to her, and with
them a number more and a young officer in command.
They were not singing now, but they all had the same
peculiar bearing so often described in our press—and
never adequately. Austerely joyous with a radiance

as of steel, proudly submissive or arrogantly obedient, with the consciousness of self-devotion, of a great descent ; rulers because they know how to be ruled. With a sense of law there was mingled the sense of adventure. Another paradox—they were pirates on the side of the law. The black flag was transformed into a black shirt, and many wore black caps crowned with bones and a death's head. And this death-like uniform had been chosen by youth, by those who sang of youth and beauty and the springtime. They were splendid and they knew it.

And the young woman who turned back on the narrow pier when she saw them coming, she too had a grandeur of her own. Too late to go on board, for in some subtle way they would make it impossible, she raised her luggage proudly and passed them without haste. Astonishing as it was, clothed in a plain black dress and an ample grey cloak, an ordinary though shapely hat concealed by her veil, both hands carrying the mean luggage, she looked at them as haughtily as they looked at her. And if there were a shade more of dignity, a more haughty gesture in the rhythm of her movements, a rhythm helped by the well-balanced weights she carried, it was when she came face to face with the young officer.

He was taller than his men, otherwise exactly like them in bearing, and in the impression he gave of high hope and enormous vitality—only the face was more intellectual : to him the Fascist adventure had perhaps a larger mental outlook. To him his previous life before this great Fascist adventure was as dim and unreal as a dream ; he could have smiled at the past self that had so little interest for him now. It was no effort to him to look as if there were no woman coming past him bearing her luggage. If he had once actually knelt before her that was in a previous state of existence. Had she tried to get on the boat he certainly would have prevented it by a glance, possibly a word to an obsequious captain. It was out of the question to allow Don Clemente's sister to sit on the same bench as his men. She was too well known as an anti-Fascist ; the effect would be bad.

Away puffed the steamer and over the water rang the voices of the Fascisti ; just for a few moments, not for too long, not like the noise of trippers who wish to be jolly, more like a brief hymn, just the early morning note.

Gemma found helpers and advisers as soon as the boat with its little crowd of blackshirts was at a safe distance. There would be another boat for Como two friendly women and an old man told her, in a couple of hours, and if there were blackshirts on that also, well then she could wait for the next. But she did not reply that Como was only the first stage of her journey ; her objective was Chiasso—she was going to join her exiled brother in Switzerland. So she thanked them and said, " Yes, yes," she would return later. " No, no," with much gratitude, she would not leave her luggage on the pier. She would not be far off, she would remain in Campo.

As Gemma went off they shrugged their shoulders and went their separate ways ; they did not talk much in Campo or in Lenno of Don Clemente or his sister.

She turned to the right and walked towards Lenno through the uninteresting hamlet of Campo. Then as the hours were passing and seeing no one coming she sat down on a big stone and dropped rather than laid the basket and the holdall on each side.

CHAPTER II

AT THE VILLA TEMPLE

IT has never been satisfactorily explained how certain cultured Englishmen who lived in Italy in the second half of last century maintained their attitude of personal superiority.

Arthur Temple was a typical case. He had come to be considered an authority on Italy in his summer visits to English country houses, much sought after by those who hoped to pay return visits to his little villa on Lake Como. In these circles he would explain Italian politics as a constitutional Liberal should ; he patronised successive Italian governments, and considered their difficulties to be due chiefly to papal intransigeance. He could say pretty hard things of Pius IX, and he could quote sincere Roman Catholic friends who agreed with him in his condemnation of Vatican policy. He also told neat little stories of Italian peasants and their lovable superstitions and quoted their phrases, which were especially applauded by those who did not like to mention that they did not understand the language. If one type of person got on his nerves more than all the other Englishmen who lived in Italy, it was the devout High Churchmen who, he declared, pretended to be more papal than the Pope.

THE SHADOW OF MUSSOLINI

When the war came Temple seemed an obvious person to assist in anti-German propaganda in Italy, but nothing much came of it. Whether this was because he was really out of touch with Italian life, or that the corroding effect of his *dolce far niente* had gone too far, no one had leisure to enquire. But he proved of real use in his own line as a charming host to British officers on sick leave, and he persevered in this hospitality without murmuring long after peace was proclaimed.

It was almost nine months after the era of Mussolini was inaugurated when he invited Rodney Castle to spend six weeks at the Villa Temple. Castle having " done all that man could " in the war with a delicate body and a peace-loving mind, had " suffered all that man must " in consequence. There were some who came back to immediate enjoyment of the peace, and Castle, happy in his chosen vocation of an Oxford don, was one. Not that he was indifferent to other men's sufferings and disappointments, far from it. But the return to intellectual life, the great amount of useful work to be done in the University and the hope of helping men of insight in the country to make it worthy of the heroes of the war—all this was absorbing. But it was not very long before he found that he was tied up in a whole network of committees, many of them academic but others of the most diverse kinds. He became overwhelmed with Reports and Agendas and Minutes and notes and proofs to a degree that left him as little time for sleep as a Carthusian and as little capacity for thought as a journalist. His nerves began to show symptoms of trouble. In the first happy return to the work he loved he had not realised that he was not yet seaworthy even for life in such a harbour. He was not sorry when he was ordered a complete rest, and he set off for Italy as pleased as a schoolboy.

Arthur Temple met him at Lenno and took him across the lake to his own villa. They were rowed over by an old Italian with a charming face who had been a young man when Temple built the villa forty years ago. Temple seeing that the man was getting old forgot that he himself was a great deal older, and the boatman never reminded him of the fact.

The Villa Temple had its own tiny harbour from which steep steps in the rock led up to the solid masonry of the house. It has been said that houses in England are built by men who expect the Last Day at an early date. But the Villa Temple like so many others on the lake seemed to be built by men who look forward as far as they can look back. The health resort of the younger Pliny will probably need houses as a health resort some two thousand years hence.

Certainly the Villa Temple seemed to intend to stay. The little boat, to Rodney Castle's regret, crossed the narrow passage of the lake only too quickly, but he was enchanted by the navigation of the tiny harbour, the crossing of its bar. A jutting rock strengthened by some mighty stone work protected one side, while the mountain rose sheer out of the water on the two others. On the upper part of these jutting rocks was the house itself.

Some twenty steps in the rock led up to the heavy door which admitted them into a hall barely furnished but impressive, not from its size, but from its appearance of strength. The charm of the thing was greatly due to its miniature proportions and its real solidity. So might children or the imaginative take it as a piece of the real fun in life.

Here then, whether out on the water or climbing leisurely, or wasting time conscientiously, Rodney came over the top of his nerve trouble. Probably the time factor had done its work in any case ; the clock had struck the hour at which he was to be well again, and he was well, but he was all the better for those days having been spent as Temple's guest. Arthur Temple had a special qualification for his work as a host in such cases. He was intensely interested in the things and in the life about him as he saw it. He still felt as if he had discovered Italy, still measured her politics and her religion from a Glad-stonian standpoint, and patronised or condemned as he had always done. But to him it was all still fresh, and, as he talked well, his English pleased Rodney and his scraps of Italian ; he was pleasant and soothing.

But on the top of the old Liberalistic notions, the quotations from Mazzini, the anecdotes of Garibaldi even, the little old English Liberal had to face the astounding coming of Mussolini. Without the least hesitation Arthur Temple took this phenomenon to his bosom, and was at once sure of two things—first

that the King of Italy was enchanted at the great
man's coming, and secondly that the Vatican would
do everything to impede his progress.

Arthur Temple had a large scrapbook which was
well known in English country houses. This year
it would have valuable additions—a whole collection
of Fascist literature and propaganda, many portraits
of Mussolini, and the old man's own sketches of
Fascisti he had seen in his neighbourhood. In
August he would have the book ready for country
house visits, when he would show it with explanations
to his entertainers and their acquaintance. In
September it would be of use in the Highlands and
later again in the south, for while other men were
out shooting partridges it would be invaluable for
amusing the ladies. How old world that sounds !
And alas ! how much fewer now were the haunts of
ancient peace where those happy visits used to be
paid. Mostly they were shut up or sold to profiteers
(whom he loved to call *pescecani* before explaining
that the word meant "sharks"). But in the old
houses that were still in the hands of distinguished
people he had lately felt that his footing was not too
sure ; if he were to keep it he must be up to date and
bring some fresh source of interest. Surely nothing
could be more up to date than Mussolini ?

There was no doubt that Rodney Castle was
interested in the portraits of Mussolini.

" I can't make the man out," he said. " Is he
posing himself, or are they making him pose and is
he half amused ? Now in this Roman Emperor stunt

with the wolf's head he looks as cruel as Nero with a bad headache, but it is plainly a make-up. Then there's the intensely earnest modern statesman with his soul full of pity for mankind looking out of his fateful eyes. Then there he is playing with a favourite lioness (the teeth drawn, one presumes), and here is the one that seems most alive, a devilish clever fellow who has been wild enough in all conscience—he almost winks at me as if I were a good fellow too and could understand—but hard as nails."

Arthur Temple fidgetted ; he found these comments irreverent.

" Whatever he is he has saved Italy from Bolshevism," he exclaimed fretfully. " People in England have no idea what things had come to. The government simply didn't govern. If the Reds ' saw red ' in any town they turned off the lights or the water or the supplies until they got their own way. Bologna, Ferrara and a dozen other towns were as much at their mercy as if there were no central government. Business simply stopped. A banker in Florence told me that the banks ceased to function. No one will ever know the number of murders, the cruelty, the misery. And then a handful of Fascists, sometimes three or four in one place, five or six in another, began the unequal fight—heroes who, alas, were too often martyrs."

Arthur Temple's little modulated voice ran up and down its small scale expressing heroic emotions as far as he could with his smooth little instrument. He was unconsciously enjoying the rehearsal for drawing-room work later on. In his lowest tones he proceeded :

" There was one poor fellow they drowned in the Arno, one of the Arditi, and when he caught hold of the boat they cut his hands off ! There was another they burnt alive. English people will never understand Fascism until they understand that Mussolini did not make a revolution—he found one in full career and made a counter-attack to save his country —he restored Italy to order. As he said himself, 'The task of the free spirit determined on the restoration of Italy is not that of revolution.' It is a fact that to most of those who understood the trend of events here the establishment of an Italian Soviet republic seemed inevitable."

That Arthur Temple had been among those who understood the trend of events was the obvious conclusion, although as a matter of fact it was not until within the last few months that he had grasped the dangers from which his hero had rescued him.

Rodney Castle was a little sceptical. His mind was tired. What he liked best was either to work at his own job—the classics—or simply to idle. He didn't want views and theories—he had had so many before the war ; neither was he looking for a great man. But although Arthur Temple's narratives sometimes seemed like a little tinkle that only tickled his attention slightly, it was different when he came to read the current Fascist literature. A few years later he maintained that that propaganda had fallen off sadly. Those first pamphlets and the early numbers of the *Gerarchia*—reports of speeches emanating from Milan—he found much of it to be great stuff. The writers were highly educated, they wrote in the most beautiful of modern languages, they meant what they said, they were ready to suffer for it ; they felt what they thought and their imaginations were in the finest state of effervescence. Beside this glorying in the new *Risorgimento*, the new life of devotion and self-sacrifice, and above all self-discipline, beside all this how material, how drab seemed the aspirations after more ease, more pay, more pleasure that had been the El Dorado promised in England to the heroes who won the war.

He began by thinking, but he kept the thought to himself for fear of hurting Temple :

" The man has an absolute genius for propaganda ; he has seen what the Germans saw, that propaganda is the machine without which a modern superman must be helpless."

Then he began to feel that no such propaganda would have been of any use without a soul within it. Was Mussolini the soul of it or did he recognise and use the souls of other people ?

There was such a peculiar combination and harmony between the classic Roman gesture, the Fascist symbolism, the surging up of the old sap that had made the Romans masters of the world, with the Christian note of hope through suffering, the ideal of self-sacrifice—the *Popolo Romano* become the *Cristiana Gente*. Those who hate their lives alone will find them, those who love life for itself must lose it. Was it the soul of the country awake at last that in desperate need of a leader, a Duce, had made the best of the only man available, or had one of the rare great geniuses of the world breathed a soul into chaos ? And if he were one of the rare great men of the world why was he not too big to play up to the endless cinema kind of celebration, the posturing of the photographer ? But have not great men, he reminded himself, in these matters condescended to be very small indeed ? If Mussolini had the habits of mind inevitable to journalism, that most degrading activity of the human intellect, did that prove that he was not born a master of men ?

Certainly there was a great trumpet note in the best of these writings, in spite of the personal adulation. After all adulation may be the natural expression of hero-worship.

It was so very long since Castle had felt any temptation to hero-worship himself ; he could no more understand it now than he could wish for a packet of sugar-plums. But some details were really absurd ! For example here was a journalist who compared the Duce to Savonarola ! Surely the type that could pose as a Roman Emperor could not also be like the Dominican friar. There was no element in Italian history that was not pressed into the service of this propaganda, but the classical was the chief note, as the name Fascisti and the Roman salute bore witness.

" Fascist," explained Temple, as he would soon be telling his women friends in England, " from the

Fasces or bundle of rods surrounding an axe which used to be carried by the Roman lictors."

Rodney smiled a little—he had heard of fasces before—but Temple went on without noticing.

" It is astonishing," he said, " what a change there has been in the appearance of the young men about here ; the war is of course at the back of it, but there's something else. One writer calls it a strange form of mimicry, but there is no doubt that a body of blackshirts might serve a sculptor for a choice of classical types. A friend of mine heard two girls in Milan agreeing that Mussolini must be right, his Fascisti were so beautiful ! And there's something in it," Temple pattered on, " for that sort of mastery and discipline comes from a man's own ideals and personal devotion to a leader. Contrast a blackshirt swinging up the road as we saw him this morning with a Prussian soldier, and you'll see what I mean."

Another time he dwelt enthusiastically on the extraordinary fact that the Fascist revolution had been almost bloodless. Then Castle had to protest :

" Why did you say the other day that it was not a revolution ? "

" Oh, you mean that Mussolini said that his spirit was not that of revolution." He paused, a little puzzled. " We want some more words even in English. He meant that he was out for construction, not destruction. No, the Fascist revolution was a revolt of law, order and sane national life against the Red International. And what I was saying," Temple liked to keep to his own thread in conversation, " the marvel is that there was so little shedding of blood. The thing that flowed instead of blood, and that still flows, is castor oil."

He thoroughly enjoyed Castle's surprise.

"Yes," he gave a little crow, "a man with the wrong views has to take a dose—so many ounces of castor oil—just enough to secure that he shall be put out of political activity for a month. After that period he will have been purged of his errors and be no longer a danger to anybody. Wasn't that an inspiration? So economical too—for the man even pays for his dose! Four lire is all he pays for his cure. Then you see if there is any mistake, as there must be in these upheavals, there are no unjust executions, while the punishment is sufficiently nasty to inspire real fear!"

On the morning of his departure Rodney wondered if they had spent one hour at the Villa Temple in which Mussolini or Fascism as an idea or the Fascists themselves had not been mentioned. There had also cropped up incidentally allusions to the Partito Popolare, who were not approved by Arthur Temple. These Christian democrats who had come to the fore since the war had according to Temple been inspired by one idea, namely to make the Vatican supreme in Italian political life. This scheme Mussolini had defeated and they were sore and difficult in consequence, though in what way they had made themselves difficult he could not explain. In this district of Como they had been supposed to be represented by a certain Don Clemente, the priest in charge of the shrine above Campo, the shrine on the heights above the famous fourteen baroque chapels. The shrine had been more crowded than ever since Don Clemente had been the preacher.

Tommaso of Lenno had reported that the priest had a magnificent voice and many words and a great way with sinners. He was no doubt, according to Temple, a dangerous influence, and whether it was true that he was exiled or not it was a good thing that he was leaving the district or perhaps already gone. His sister, the Signora Gemma, had probably returned by now to Florence, her native city. Temple had seen her once coming down the Campo path, a beautiful woman, but what had impressed him most was the energy and dignity of her bearing as she came down the steep cobbled pathway which he found to be almost impossible. "She made me think of the wonderful Florentine ladies whom we admire as they intrude into the most sacred scenes of many a fifteenth century fresco."

That was the only allusion that was made to Gemma, and had not Castle been thrown across her path after that he would certainly not have remembered her existence.

CHAPTER III

MAKING FOR THE FRONTIER

TEMPLE prided himself on his arrangements for speeding his parting guests and he followed his usual plan with Rodney. First they were rowed over to Lenno, and there Tommaso, who kept a motor for hire, was to be in waiting to drive to Chiasso, so that the journey proper would only start at the frontier. This time they were in Lenno before Tommaso was ready, so they strolled along almost the whole short way to Campo. Arthur Temple never walked fast, he liked to dawdle and to chat.

"Before I came to Italy," he said, "I used to imagine that the children in great Italian art were the conceptions of genius, but now I realise that those little cherubs and glorious boys were realistic portraits. Look at that group now! But, good gracious! there is the Signora Gemma, Don Clemente's sister, sitting by the roadside and looking as if she were a figure of fate come off the ceiling of the Sistine Chapel. We had better not disturb her."

Rodney Castle ventured his own opinion : "She looks as if she needed help of some sort."

"I would not intrude. I don't know her." Temple spoke a little testily, and insisted on turning back into the tunnel on the road to Lenno.

" Ah, here comes the car—lucky fellow! A glorious drive before you. I suppose you will get to Chiasso in a couple of hours."

They parted very warmly, and indeed Temple had been very kind to Rodney. He liked being kind to young men whose health had suffered from the war, and Castle had proved to be a most interesting and pleasant guest

Rodney had no time to lose; indeed the motor should have followed him sooner. But as he came out of the tunnel there was still the lady sitting on the stone and now he acted on his own impulse. He stopped the motor close by her, jumped out and bowed :

" Do you understand English ? "

" Yes." She bowed a little stiffly.

" Have you missed the steamer ? Can I give you a lift towards Como ? I am going to Chiasso."

" Chiasso ! " The transformation of her face was extraordinary. The rather large features were curiously mobile in expression, and from woe to joy the change was instantaneous. Of all the departures the village could have imagined for Signora Gemma that of driving away in a motor with a fine young Englishman was the most astonishing. Of the effect produced, the food for gossip she was providing, Gemma was profoundly unconscious—her mind was full of anxiety as to the wisdom of her proceeding— the doubt whether she was acting fairly to her rescuer. She was also feeling rather faint and confused.

MAKING FOR THE FRONTIER

Rodney Castle was observant.

" Have you had any food to-day ? " was his first question of this impressive young woman by his side.

" No, why should I ? It is quite early."

" Is it Como or Chiasso you want to go to ? "

" Oh," she said, " speak low. Tommaso may hear you. Do you know who I am ? "

" Yes, I have heard of you. I will speak very quietly, Tommaso shall not hear. Is it Chiasso ? "

" Yes."

" You want to leave the country and you fear they will stop you ? "

" Yes, yes."

" The brutes ! "

She gave a little shrug : " It is bigger than all that."

Her English accent like that of most Italians was attractive, so different from their French accent, than which nothing can be more ugly ; also her voice was resonant and it held Rodney from the first.

" But to bully women ! " he cried.

" It is a vast reaction," she said calmly, " courage that has been born of fear, not calm stable courage. However they have routed the devils out of many high places ; but you are English, you know the Bible, you have read of how devils return ? "

She leant back wearily and he thought she was going to faint.

" I have some wine," he said tentatively. A countrywoman of his own would not have dared to touch wine before anything else had crossed her lips.

THE SHADOW OF MUSSOLINI

When he produced a straw-covered bottle, intended for luncheon while waiting at the frontier, and a piece of bread, she dipped the bread in the wine and took it grateful but unsmiling—whereas Englishwomen always smile when they are provided for. Then she began to talk quickly, almost monotonously; the note of emotion seemed on the same key, to him a mysterious one :

"Our friends had more courage. Because liberty was abused they did not desert her. The giovinezza of this country were in the hands of the devil ; the Partito Popolare won many of them to Christian freedom ; we did not think that one tyranny could only be met by another."

"And now your leader is in exile ? " exclaimed Rodney indignantly.

"Yes." She gave a comprehensive glance at the glories all about them, as the road lay on the lakeside. "Exiled from this Italy," she said in a low voice.

Then they passed into a tunnel and for the rest of the way until near to the town of Como there were frequent alternations between glorious scenic effects of lake and mountain and the deep cool tunnels made by the men who blast the rocks even for us in England. There are Italians, a curious lost legion, entirely devoted to the work, who may be found making tunnels anywhere the world over, who pierce through any obstacle if they cannot remove it.

"What do you think will happen at the frontier ? " asked Rodney presently.

"I think it will be all right, only I had word last

night that unless I got off by the first boat I might not get off at all, and that no motor would take me. When I saw the Fascisti going on board I knew it would be no use—and the captain signalled to me. That is how things are done, are made impossible. They will not take the odium of what you call bullying a woman, but no one would dare to befriend me. Heaven help a country with such liberators ! But I think I will get by at Chiasso because no one knows me there, and I have not the surname of my brother Clemente. I don't think direct orders will be given. Only, my unknown benefactor, you kind Englishman, if there is a blackshirt on the small station there may be found that there is some irregularity in my passport. That will be all." She laughed.

Rodney Castle told her his name and something of his history.

" I want to go to England," she said. " I do not believe in staying in Switzerland. England alone is safe."

" But you will be glad enough to get into Switzerland to-day," he laughed.

Suddenly her face changed from ironic smiles to simple tragedy, and those changes as he came to know her better had a constant interest for him. They were not April sun and shower although they were as swift ; they were more like thunder clouds and the rifts made by the light behind.

" May it please God," and the contralto notes deepened the impression.

35

Rodney was becoming anxious : " When and where did you get your passport ? "

" Quite recently in Milan."

" Which class will you travel ? "

" Oh, third." She was surprised at the question.

They were nearing the point where the road branched off towards Chiasso, leaving Como on the left.

" Which would be best," he said, " for me to take our tickets and keep our luggage together ? "

" Oh yes, please, if you do not mind."

Castle did not mind, because he was entirely bent on getting his new acquaintance out of Italy, but he was not unaware of difficulties for himself that might ensue.

" How about Tommaso ? " he asked.

" Oh, he belongs body and soul to Mr. Temple, who always hires from him. Have no fear of him. He lives in Lenno and he knows me though he pretends not to to-day, but you are a friend of Mr. Temple's, he won't get you into trouble—*sicuro*."

Chiasso seemed sound asleep when they reached it after a long bit of uninteresting country. Fortunately Temple's favourite had often driven his guests to the frontier and had had more than once to rouse the stationmaster and the porter from their slumbers.

Rodney was alarmed at the noise that ensued on this occasion. The chauffeur disappeared in the stationmaster's office, and then two men out of sight joined in such an altercation with such a tremendous

36

flow of language that he was alarmed for fear that they had already seen his companion. And when they emerged on the platform their appearance confirmed his fears. Fury was depicted on their countenances and expressed in violent gestures, while Tommaso also appeared to be beside himself with anger. Rodney was desperately perplexed as to what the row was about and when the combatants would come to blows.

Presently they flung themselves on Castle's luggage and in an outburst of rage the second official pointed with scorn to one suitcase which Rodney meekly unlocked. With an attitude of superb contempt they glanced at the contents and then began chalking everything, including even Gemma's little lot. Gemma meanwhile had taken refuge in the waiting-room.

Then came the question of the passports. Rodney left the stationmaster and the chauffeur still in violent quarrel and summoned Gemma to the passport office, where a magnificent official was enjoying a quiet smoke. He hardly glanced at their passports before stamping them, and then the formalities seemed to be safely finished. Quite suddenly too, the storm ceased that had raged between Tommaso and the stationmaster and the porter. Tommaso having received Rodney's ample pay retired to his motor with satisfaction and the rest moved to the gate that divided the Italian side of the station from the Swiss.

Just as they reached the barrier Rodney found

Gemma had fallen behind him and turning to let her pass he saw a tall young man in a black shirt at the other end of the platform. Two things struck him at that anxious moment, that the man was a fine young fellow and that he had a damned lot of swagger.

In a voice not shouting but resonant came an order and the stationmaster turned in obsequious fear. But as had been obvious enough the young man who inspired such terror had arrived too late.

Gemma was in Switzerland.

The stationmaster hastened to meet the Fascist. He drew a paper out of his pocket and held it out :

" I had orders to let her go," he said.

" A good riddance," said the blackshirt carelessly. He did not add, " And I had orders to frighten her that she may not come back."

CHAPTER IV

The Eternal Snows

It did not occur to either Rodney or Gemma that they could do the rest of the journey apart. As luck would have it they found a little half compartment at the end of a carriage empty. It held four seats and but one had been taken and on it at present were only a coat and an attaché case.

As soon as they were settled and Rodney had disposed of their small baggage above their heads he asked Gemma to explain the violent quarrel at the station, which although he knew Italian fairly well, he had quite failed to understand.

" Ah, dear Tommaso," she said with an affectionate smile. " He provoked that quarrel for our sakes. He brought all our luggage on to the platform to annoy the porter and he roused the master of the station from his siesta. So they were far too angry with him to notice us. It was good on the part of Tommaso. And what a narrow escape ! After this the frontier will be more carefully guarded."

Rodney enjoyed Tommaso's amazing power of showing rage.

" Oh, he felt it too," Gemma explained. " Probably it is an old quarrel—and ours is a grand language for a quarrel, let alone the gestures."

She looked much brighter.

"Strange that I feel less like an exile at this moment than like a schoolgirl who has taken a holiday without leave! It is partly because this journey has usually been the beginning of my holiday. Domen' Iddio alone knows how long this one will be! And partly because if I had been sent back now; well, it would have been an awful life! And I owe this to you! Let me just thank you."

She turned round to him and for a moment Rodney was startled by such unexpected brightness, a spiritual brightness that shone out of her dark eyes. No eyes have that peculiar brightness that have not at some time shed many tears. The light that shone at that moment seemed to consecrate the day's adventure, seemed to give Rodney a sense of responsibility towards her which the briefness of their acquaintance made almost absurd.

As the train mounted the heights of the mighty barrier between Italy and the rest of Europe their thoughts were turned towards Gemma's beloved country.

"But to live there," she said, "suspected, hated by just those who have loved us. How could I bear it? To see them, our beloved giovinezza, our youth, full of false hopes, dazzled by a sinister light, all the beauty and joy of their lives given over to a great delusion! They were so hungry for the ideal! The war had brought out such great heroic characters and it seemed as if the virtues, the powers the war had evoked, were to die for want of the atmosphere in which they could exist. Many, frantic at the wrongs of our civilisation, were drawn into the ranks of the Reds. You English cannot imagine what life had become in our country. You who look on Italy as an inn, as d'Annunzio said, an inn painted with bright colours against an indigo blue sky and picturesque peasants, little know what a hell it was becoming ! The Pope had only given permission to vote in the elections on the eve of the war. So all the political parties were anti-clerical. Then a noble group of Catholics with Don Sturzo at their head undertook to organise the Catholic vote. As the war ended the Partito Popolare sprang into being and in a couple of years had over a hundred seats in the Chamber. Don Sturzo was the guide and the organising genius, his was the voice that roused the Catholic youth of the country. We offered them the ideals of a Christian democracy, of a true *Risorgimento*, of liberty, of decentralisation ; we saw the country sinking under the Red tyranny but we did not despair of liberty. We believed in constitutional government such as you have in England. If it succeeds with you, why not with us ? "

Rodney listening eagerly felt with a spasm of honesty that this passion of admiration for the British Constitution as it now exists hardly appealed to him as she evidently believed it must. But she was only silent for a moment. As she told him later in the day she had been very lonely of late. To-day she was free, and relieved of the fear of meeting at any moment old friends turned into foes. The desire to make this Englishman understand her point of view, the hope of justifying her brother and his friends, caused an outpouring of freedom of speech which appeared to him absolutely natural because it was so spontaneous.

" Ah," she went on after a moment's silence, " we were so near success. If our leader had had only true men under him we should have swept the country, we should have held our own against the Reds. Then there would have been no need for a counter-revolution, for bombs and beatings and the puerile bestiality of castor oil."

Rodney succeeded in not smiling but it was hard not to. The immense ingenuity of the medicinal cure for the wrong views of opponents had greatly taken his fancy, but he was almost ashamed of being amused in the face of her earnestness.

" They took from us the ideal of a new moral life for Italy, they took from us the crusade for self-sacrifice as opposed to self-making, to materialism. They used the fires we had enkindled in the hearts of men all over Italy, and they used men's souls to climb into power ! Has it not been so in hundreds of places as well as at Lenno. At Lenno the beautiful glorious giovinezza became inspired by our ideals, and now the ' flame ' as they call him, the ' tyrant ' as history will call him, has lured them by the same notes we struck in their hearts : service for their country, unselfishness, work—only they worship the ideal of nationality and we worshipped Christ and the freedom wherewith He has made us free."

THE ETERNAL SNOWS

Rodney felt deeply moved by the last words dropped in a low tone as if half to herself. To him this last idea held a great appeal. He and his contemporaries at Oxford had also dreamt of this great notion of a civilisation predominantly Christian. And then when he was most eager to hear more, a large, burly, fair, smiling German seemed to occupy the whole carriage, as he claimed his seat.

They were on the great heights of the Alps, and the train was moving almost on level ground between the peaks, when Rodney and Gemma were left alone again. They could see the large German in the corridor at a safe distance smoking his pipe.

" One can feel the snow now," said Gemma in a voice of awe. " Here they still talk Italian, presently it will be German." She shrugged her shoulders. " They would not teach me German at the convent because of Austria." She laughed. " They were Venetians, and my people are Florentines."

" They taught you English admirably. Did they also teach you French and Latin ? "

" Yes, they were good linguists and good women, but they taught me too many pieties and too little doctrine, and so I lost both one and the other. But I am inclined to blame them where I ought only to blame myself."

She was silent, but the circumstances were too much for her natural reticence. It is often from complete strangers, to be met once and forgotten, that it is easy to seek sympathy. A kind human face, courtesy, the fellowship of youth, the accident of what might have proved a real adventure together, opened the floodgates of speech. With all this Gemma must either have withdrawn forcibly into herself or have let her overburdened mind have its relief.

" You are a Protestant ? " she asked.

" No—an Anglican—perhaps something of a modernist ; rather indifferent, I fear."

" Ah 'Modernista!'" she exclaimed, " but that is not to be indifferent, only to be confused."

Rodney laughed. " Have you always been a Catholic ? "

" I have been an Atheist, a Communist. But I did not play at Catholicism without dogma and without authority. I went what you so gracefully call the whole hog. Now that was exciting. Of course," she smiled very sadly, " my mother thought me a lost soul and she was quite right. We are all born rebels, and to be a rebel against love and truth is to be a low, mean, ugly thing, very low," she repeated sadly, " very mean, very ugly. But we had great temptations, the girls of my set. My mother wanted me to lead a stifled existence according to the conventionalities of her class, my father would have allowed me some degree of liberty, but, although he did not agree, he did not interfere, and so there it was! I met my Cæsare, a Socialist, a Nihilist who had never known better things, and I became consumed with his ideals. I went to work in an office for Socialist propaganda where Cæsare was a leading spirit, and where, God forgive us, we both looked for guidance to the journalist, Benito Mussolini. In the May of the fatal year 1914 we were married. Well, war was declared, and I, with rather more important people, was a Pacifist. From the time war was declared Cæsare was restless, unsettled. He was a poet, his poems are well known now, he made no money with them then, but I knew what they were worth—-well, his poems began to change and I was alarmed.

" Then he went to Lenno to a great Socialist gathering, and the evening he came back he asked me to walk up with him to San Miniato. The sun was just on its downward way when we started, and it was flaring red into the Arno as we came back. We were very silent as we climbed the steep narrow path that led on to the piazza in front of the church. And from there we looked down on our beloved Florence, the Duomo, the Baptistery, the winding Arno and its bridges—ah me ! all that I may very likely never see again. No one can realise Florence, the Florence of Dante and Savonarola, who has not looked upon it from San Miniato. And there he told me, ' Mussolini has declared for war and I am with him.' You know," Gemma turned to Rodney, " that Mussolini was then only a brilliant journalist, a leader among the Socialists. He had been the leading pacifist and now I felt furious at the change. I had the self-command to be silent at least for some

45

minutes. ' Ah,' he said, ' I wish you had been with me. I wish you had seen him facing all that raging crowd. A little man, just an editor whose whole reputation rests on his Socialist propaganda, whose living depends on their buying his paper. After he had told them it was a just war, a resistance to tyranny, when he said that Italy would be untrue to her past if she stood aside, I thought they might have killed him. What do you think he did, Gemma ? I waited anxiously for a lull. I knew they wanted him to speak, if only to condemn him out of his own mouth, and when the lull came, he took my breath away. He spoke like a furious master, their little editor, and he threatened them with punishment. ' I shall not forgive you,' he said. ' I shall make you suffer for this.' If there had been legions at his command outside, he could not have been one iota firmer. Ah me ! " she gave a groan, " as I tell this story to you, an Englishman, you do not feel as I do the monstrous shadow of a tyrant already. I think it was a moment of second sight, the awful predominance of one ego. ' I shall punish. I shall not forgive.' " She shuddered. " When Cæsare had finished I began. He was amazed to find that I who had fed on his thoughts, eaten out of his hand as they say, dared to have an opinion of my own. I tried to make him see that it was his own thoughts— what he had taught me himself—that I was bringing up against him, that I merely abounded in his own sense. It was no use—there was a light in his eye, a beauty in his face as I quarrelled with him I had never seen before. I made him angry. I made him cold and hard and impossible. At least so he appeared to me. I learnt afterwards that he suffered torments that evening. Then, when I had beaten in vain against the rock of his will, he told me he was going to fight the moment Italy declared war. And then I recognised that it was just to save him personally that I had put up this fight. Had he subconsciously known it too ? He was of the poet nature, imaginative, pure, fanciful, naturally ascetic. A man of action would have been more open to a woman's influence, he had no difficulty in resisting me.

" He became one of the Arditi and he died on the eternal snows."

Rodney watched her as she raised her face to the heights ; the train had come closer to the mountain range and the white peaks appeared absolutely inaccessible. He thought she had ended there, but presently she went on—

" But there were a few weeks before the end—a great interval—for in the silence of the heights he chose Christ for his King, he sought for the highest and he found Christ. He wanted to satisfy his hunger for God and he found that the only way was for him to belong to the God-Man, to be a member of his mystical body. My brother Clemente reached him three times on impossible positions, and there far from our world they were near to the other. Clemente told me, and he knows about these things, that Cæsare passed into spiritual heights with very unusual rapidity. ' He taught me more than I could teach him,' Clemente said. His lungs had been delicate, but he was astonishingly well on his hard duty. His death was just an accident." She was silent again before she went on—

" What I knew already Clemente told me afterwards—those two who loved me talked much of me together. I was stubborn; no circumstances, no influences of head or heart, can bring us back to God of themselves. Even after he had died, my Cæsare, I did not seem to be changed. I was like ice; I could not find any sympathy or help. I wanted Clemente to tell me far more than he could about Cæsare, and then I hurt him by the way I took what he did say. I looked on Catholicism as small, tyrannical and mean. I said that Christianity and liberty must go together—and then I heard of Don Sturzo and I persuaded Clemente to go and see him. They became friends, and to Don Sturzo he said :

" ' If my sister cannot be a Catholic without being a Liberal must I not allow to her that she is within her rights ? ' And from me he looked out to others like me and through my soul he saw the need of many souls. I was attracted by all I heard from Clemente of the priest of genius and sanctity with his extraordinary personal distinction, ' the little long-nosed priest of genius,' as Mussolini is reported to have called Don Sturzo. I went to see him, and instead of talking of liberty he spoke sternly though very gently of the needs of my soul. I was annoyed, but how right he was ! Not long after that I went out to hear Clemente preach to the troops in the open.

THE ETERNAL SNOWS

I can hear even now his glorious voice passing in waves of sound to the extreme limits of the men massed about him. It was the first time I had heard the preaching of the Cross to men who had to suffer, perhaps to die for such as me, who could not fight, and for the first time I knew that Christ who had died for me and for them had bought us for Himself by the shedding of blood. But I learnt that lesson less from what Clemente said than from the men themselves. Their uplifted faces were a revelation to me, the revelation of my own sinfulness, for how innocent of soul were these men compared to me ! It is so hard for those who have no gross temptations to see the ugliness of their own sins. I understood suddenly how little their sins had poisoned the souls of these poor fellows, this fodder for the cannon. How low, how corrupt, how selfish my soul was compared to theirs. It would háve been far better for the moral state of the world had I died for one of them than that one of them should die for me. *Animae naturaliter Christianae,* they had not debauched their highest faculties. Sins of the intellect roused the wrath of Christ more than sins of the flesh ; it is the corruption of the highest that is actually the lowest. The Pharisees, may we say it in all reverence, seem to have got upon His nerves ! So the faces of our soldiers drinking in Clemente's ' foolishness of preaching ' showed me the wisdom of God. I had resisted even Cæsare's letters, even his dying message, but that evening when I got back to Florence I knelt for hours in Santa Maria Novella."

CHAPTER V

The Sincerity of Mussolini

The day was not spent entirely without food or rest. Rodney's basket, generously supplied at the Villa Temple, gave them lunch and they rested in the great tunnel, but at length the wish for tea drove them to the restaurant car that was by then almost empty. The move, the presence of the waiter, the click of the cups all changed the atmosphere. It was inevitable that as soon as Gemma ceased to speak of herself they should again discuss Mussolini. Rodney plunged into the questions that Arthur Temple would not answer, and he demanded crudely to be told if Mussolini was genuine and sincere. Instantly there was a change in Gemma's bearing. She leant back and swept the board as it were with her hand :
" Genuine, yes genuine enough ! "
" But really sincere ? "
" Yes, sincere enough, *Dio lo sa !* "
" But does he mean what he says ? "
" Of course he does. What should he mean ? "
Rodney was baffled.
" The question is," said Gemma, " what does he say ? Surely he says plainly enough : ' I am your master and your only one. You were slaves of the Red Terror and therefore I am your liberator. You

50

could not sow or reap or buy or sell. Your houses, your workshops were insanitary, you needed bridges, you needed water and light, and when you asked for these things the government that had courage for nothing else had the courage to refuse them to you. I will give you light and water and drains, and you shall be rich, and Italy will once more take her place among the nations.' "

" And he has done all this ! " exclaimed Rodney. " It could never have been done without him."

" But no, a thousand times no ! " exclaimed Gemma, her face flushed, and her whole bearing an indignant protest. " It would have been done without him. The Partito Popolare had started the work and was doing it very well, but he got all the credit."

Then without stopping to prove her point as to the reforms made by the popular party she went on :

" Ah, he is clever that one ! He saw which way the wind was blowing, he saw that the Socialists had been defeated by the war. Who was a more vehement pacifist than Mussolini until he saw which side was going to win ? Then he threw himself into the war, but he remained a Red until he again saw the signs of the times. Ah, he is the greatest of weather pro-phets, I will allow him that ! He saw that he had no chance of being a Lenin, because Italy did not want a Lenin, so he came in on top of the reaction towards law and order ! He exploited the great virtues born of the war."

Then Rodney told her what he felt about the

propaganda he had been studying ; he quoted a fine article from the *Gerarchia* on the need not only for the great pagan virtues, law, order, discipline, submission to fate, but for the more Christian note of hope and self-sacrifice, of self-discipline as a means of self-development not stagnation.

She leant back while he was speaking, her eyes half shut in an attitude of supreme patient scorn. Before long he ran down, indeed it was difficult to keep it up, but he had got out his main question :

" How had this journalist adventurer, whose youth did not furnish a pleasant record, come by the ethos, the moral atmosphere of Fascism ? Surely if he were the soul of this enterprise he must have a great soul himself."

" How did he come by it ? " cried Gemma. " He stole it. His own soul ! " she shrugged her shoulders. " Hell alone knows what has become of his own soul ! But there was his supreme power of seeing what was coming. He stepped in just in time to prevent a great Catholic movement of social reconstruction. We were at last free to take our part in the life of the country. Catholics had been bound to inaction by those above them ; they were set free at the psychological moment when they were really needed. We of the Partito Popolare it was who knew that the virtues born of the war must be preserved in our public life if Italy were not to go under. We struck the note of hope of a Christian *Risorgimento* and at once our party grew by leaps and bounds, and then Mussolini threw over Socialism, took our war cries, stole our sacred fire and exploited the souls we had roused from a deadly sleep. Only he was far more astute, he neglected no element that could appeal to different sections of the people. He always gets the credit for the things he has borrowed. All that black shirt nonsense and the salutes and the whole outward show of Fascism was really from the man of operatic vision, d'Annunzio. Mussolini was the Liberator to those who loved liberty, the Duce, the Master, to those who hated chaos ; he was as self-sacrificing as a Christian martyr and he gave power and position in the name of asceticism and self-denial to all who took service under him. But the cleverest thing of all is his attitude to the Vatican. He said more than once years ago that anti-clericals were fools, and he had declared war also long ago on the Freemasons who might have stood in his upward way. If he had gone cap in hand and knelt before the Pope he would have lost as much as he gained. He did not go to Canossa, but he did just the one thing to gain the Pope's heart, he allowed the Crucifix back into the schools. The journalist who had been expelled from Lausanne for a speech in which he had exalted Buddha and belittled Christ gave Italian children his permission to be educated as Christians ! And with that he won the Vatican and the sympathy of Catholics not only throughout the country, but throughout the whole world. He is too clever to underestimate the Black International, the one world influence that has survived all the attacks, and he knows what these attacks are worth. Besides, he also recognises that religion is useful, is necessary for national life. 'Italy needs a religion,' you will find it said in one of the Fascist articles. 'She must have a religion united in itself, with deep roots in the past, her own past. She must have an undoubted authority.' Obviously there is only one religion that answers the description. And so he won the position he needed in the eyes of the religious world without sheer hypocrisy. There are convents in Italy where you can hear wonderful accounts of his prayers and penances, and how he insists on all the babies in Italy being baptized, and how he administers castor oil to atheists, and how all the Freemasons are trying to murder him ! He put back the Crucifixes, made his bow to the Church, and their vivid imaginations have supplied the details."

" Frightfully clever," said Castle in a dubious tone. He could not, even listening to Gemma, forget that her account was not entirely unprejudiced. And then, as she found she had struck no answering chord, it appeared to him that she fell suddenly from the mood of conviction and trust in her own power of carrying conviction to others to the opposite condition. After all she was running away from the new régime, she who belonged to the defeated party ; was it likely that in face of the material success of Fascism strangers would listen to the truth when she spoke it ? A terrible sense of loneliness and desolation seemed to come over her. Probably she had believed she could do more for her friends out of Italy than in it. But even this friendly Englishman, who was not pro-Mussolini, who had helped her to get across the frontier, clearly was not only not influenced by her, but felt her to be so prejudiced as to provoke reaction.

Rodney, in the interest of his enquiry, had felt less sympathy, had become more critical. After a few moments' silence he would have attempted—a fatal attempt—an argument that might bring out more information. But looking up he saw the face opposite to him transformed. There was no longer the sense of magnificent tragedy felt but not overwhelming, there was now a quivering, a burden of suffering that was almost unbearable. The great dark eyes were liquid and terribly fervent, and large tears shone clearly on the olive cheeks that had lost the beautiful flush he had admired in the morning. She looked absolutely alone, desolate, without strength. He was not sorry to move again, back to their little compartment.

They had passed out of Italian Switzerland and were nearing Andermatt, while the greatness of the scenery, the mighty mountains to the east and the west, seemed to occupy them both. They were silent, but it was the silence of a tacitly avowed intimacy, not of embarrassment or of dryness. While they were content with silence Rodney Castle felt, as he had felt among mountains before, as if he could hear a mighty chant rising from the inaccessible heights— nature's psalm from nature's monasteries—and as if the train made no noise at all. But soon there came a change, and it seemed as if the train made all the noise of the world, and the snow-covered heights and the pinewoods held in sacred charge all its silence.

As they came nearer the lake their eyes no longer wandered to the east. They became as anxious to see down into the depths of that most austere of all the lakes in its middle part as to see the great woods above on the lower ranges of mountains, up to the dominant horizontal lines of the peaks. The awful glories of the scene brought them very near together. Rodney felt the whole day to have been like a great rhythmic curve, full of beauty, of action, of a gradual revelation. It seemed ever so long ago that he had heard Arthur Temple twaddle on about Mussolini and the Vatican, and large views, and picturesque superstitions—twaddle Rodney had actually enjoyed. And now he was sitting next to Gemma looking on this immense pageant through those eyes that seemed so much more actually beautiful than he had supposed only a few hours ago. There were blue shadows round those eyes, but there was absolutely no self-consciousness in them, no knowledge of the loneliness of her soul, of her purity, of her pride. She looked at him with kindness :

"We shall be in Lucerne very soon, in the town of hotels and toys. We shall probably not meet again. You have done as much for me since we left my country as you did in helping me to escape. Thank you."

"But where are you going to stay? Can't I help you at all?"

"I am going up to a hotel in the woods at Gütsch.

I have been there before. I shall go up by the little funicular railway."

" I know the Pension," said Rodney with business-like promptitude. " I shall take you there."

Clearly Gemma did not like this proposition, but Rodney was not at the moment at all unselfish. He wanted to go with her and he meant to go with her. She gave way a little haughtily just before the tunnel that ends in the station at Lucerne.

CHAPTER VI

THE SECRET LETTER

THERE was considerable confusion on the platform as Rodney and Gemma got down from the train, and he was sorry he had not registered his luggage at Chiasso. There were now five things to compete with—three of his own and two of Gemma's. He had a firm grip on Gemma's shabby possessions, so as to be sure that she could not escape him while he sought for a porter. As he went impatiently on his quest he thought he saw a face he knew, not really familiar to him but a face with some unpleasant association attached to it. It was a man in a heavy coat trimmed with common fur and a large shabby Trilby hat pulled down over the eyes. The man had dirty, well-shaped hands, and these latter cleared up his doubts. Of course he was a Russian, a prisoner in Germany who for some reason or other had turned up in Oxford after the war. Some undergraduate had tried to arouse Rodney's interest by saying that this unsavoury personage knew all about Russia. Rodney had declined to meet him ; he had seen him at a distance and that was enough to show that he was as ugly as he was dirty, and he was sure his mind needed washing as much as his body. It was intolerable in this dreadful station to see this noxious reptile. It was bad enough to have fallen from Heaven on to a mixed crowd of tourists with a predominating German element, but to see this dirty brute as well was intolerable.

He found a porter and turned to bring him back towards the carriage. He blinked at that moment, as a man does who is incredulous of his own eyes, for he saw this Russian animal, while passing rather roughly close to Gemma as if he did not see that she was there, give her a letter. And Gemma, who did not seem aware of his existence, actually took the letter from him !

Rodney was not a good actor—he was far too ceremoniously polite while still under the shock of what he had seen. He directed the porter to put his own luggage in the cloakroom and followed Gemma to the tramway still bearing her basket and her holdall. There was a group of English people outside the station, and for the first time he felt it a little absurd that he should be carrying this mean little lot of luggage.

The tram rattled along the street by the river, past the covered bridges on their right and what was once the Jesuit church on their left. With his extreme politeness they had fallen silent and embarrassed. He knew she had wished that he would not get into the tram, but now temper made him determined to go on and he was glad if that annoyed her. Gemma had never seen an Englishman in a temper like this but she knew when a man was past reason as well as anyone. They got out as the tram stopped by the tiny station of the water railway up the Gütsch hill.

Rodney took their tickets and they passed on to the absurd little platform and looked up at the toy railway. The up carriage and the down were just passing each other midway on the steep ascent, they had but three minutes to wait. Anybody might have taken them for a man and wife or for lovers in a quarrel, and they were neither. The day's adventure did not in the least excuse his attitude, though his attitude might excuse the awful haughtiness of hers.

When the carriage touched the bottom of the line she got in before he could help her, and then he lifted in her luggage and got in himself. A Roman chariot would have suited their bearing better than the absurd little carriage that was noisily emptying its load of water into the tank. Who has not enjoyed that brief ascent between the little bright trees in the clear atmosphere, with an increasing view at every moment of the civilised sunny smooth end of the lake of Lucerne, and the range of mountains beyond ?

The few minutes in the little railway seemed neither long nor short to these two, only conscious of their mutual dreadful wrath. Still immensely polite he got out at the top and followed Gemma as she passed into the great pinewood. It is impossible to suppress the comparison of that entrance into the wood to the entrance into a Cathedral. The hot sun left behind, the fragrance, the cool, the roof overhead, the smooth brown ground under their feet.

Rodney suddenly felt ashamed of his own wrath. He wished vehemently that she would stay there, in that sanctuary, and give him time to recover— to apologise, to do something or other ! There must surely be some way back to the unity, the peace, of that day together. But Gemma seemed to have forgotten the existence of her voluntary porter. She stood for one moment looking at the great fir trees, drew a deep breath ending in a sharp sigh, and then turned quickly to the right and followed a little brown path between the trunks. There on a tree was fixed a gaudily painted board announcing with a pointing hand the way to the Pension Victoria : it was new and shiny with varnish. In any case a board in that spot was a desecration. A hundred yards of the little path brought them to a small gate amid bushes where an invisible dog was growling.

Then Gemma turned towards Rodney and held out her hand. Their eyes met for the first time since his wrath had first flared up and for a moment they saw each other's sudden tears well up, though sternly forbidden to overflow.

Then, Castle having gained just so much to hoard and treasure in the days to come, they were interrupted. A tall, rough, sinister-looking man emerged from the gate, said something guttural to Gemma and took the luggage from Rodney, who mechanically let it go. He thought that she said ' good-bye,' and then she went through the gate followed by the burly unkempt Pension servant carrying the basket and the holdall. His large figure hid her from sight.

Rodney went back to Lucerne station and took his own luggage out of the cloakroom.

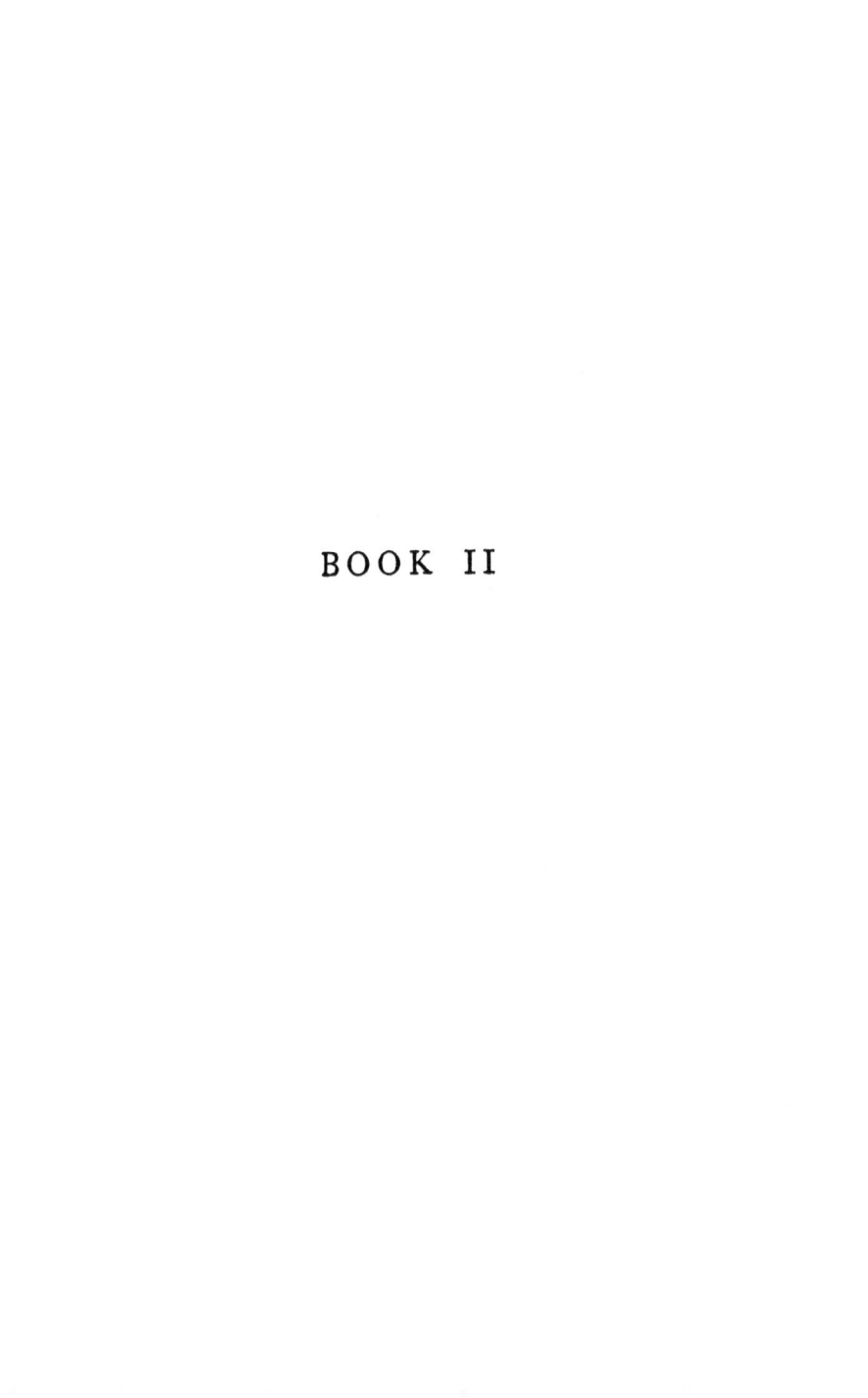

BOOK II

CHAPTER I

Lady Lavington is Annoyed

Quite the sanest people are not always responsible for their actions. Rodney did an impossible thing that same evening, a thing he could not have done before or after. He had told Arthur Temple that he hoped to find the Lavingtons at Lucerne, he knew they had intended to be there just then—after which Temple had charged him with many messages. He did not decide to stop at Lucerne precisely in order to meet the aunt and niece, Lady Lavington and Patsey Lavington, but he had really counted not a little on the prospect, and had that morning planned to seek them at the Schweizerhof after dinner.

Then as the journey went on he entirely forgot these friends in Gemma's company, and by the time he had parted from her and returned to the station to get his luggage out of the cloakroom, he had not given a thought to how he would spend the evening, or indeed where he would dine.

He had written to engage a room at one of the less crowded hotels recommended by Arthur Temple, and the porter having read the labels on his suitcases asked if he should take them there or whether he should call a taxi.

Rodney said he would walk, and the porter after

they had crossed the bridge chose the pavement on the left so that they passed close under the windows of the principal hotels facing the lake. The man moved quickly and Rodney stalked after him swinging his stick, his eyes fixed on the pavement, until, as the devil would have it, he looked straight in at the windows of the Schweizerhof. He saw perfectly well a small round table at which were seated three people—Lady Lavington, Patsey and an elderly man unknown to him. It was a picture that would have charmed most men and women. At other tables sat women who were too fat, who had too much paint, and too many jewels, and not enough clothes, whose voices were loud, whether shrill or harsh. Here were two English ladies, his ideal of what was truly delightful. Lady Lavington was still a beautiful woman, and Patsey had something that no one else had : the way she held herself, the slightest difference in her eyes with their beautiful straight glance, the touch of sarcasm in the smile lost in the grave rich kindness of the whole face at rest.

A month ago, a week ago, no, twenty-four hours ago, with what pleasure he would have recognised the slim figure, the thin little hand holding a cigarette crooked, the mass of soft hair. He knew so well the impression she gave of energy ignoring fatigue, for she was not really strong, with the peculiar combination of enjoyment and sympathy. And to-night he was deadly incapable of any sense of pleasure at all : the little table in the light, the flowers and the champagne bottle annoyed him. The three figures were all so easily placed in such a different world. Probably he really was incapable of passing from the influences of the day in time to mind his manners. Fate and Gemma really were too much for him. Anyhow, whether he was to blame or not, having plainly betrayed that he had seen them, he passed on pretending that he had not. It had been a long stare, not a hasty glance—that was the trouble !

Lady Lavington gave a startled look at Patsey, who was in close attention to the man of the party— General Sir John Decey—and in his conversation she remained to his delight completely absorbed until they went upstairs to bed.

The aunt and niece parted after a brief good-night, but Lady Lavington remained standing in the middle of her room irresolute. If it had been one of her other nieces she would probably have gone into her room, or any one of them would probably have come into hers. Anyhow, somebody would have said :

" Did you see Rodney Castle ? "

" Yes, and he saw us."

Different things would have followed according to which of the other girls it had been, but Patsey would have a wall of impenetrable silence. It was very uncomfortable. Rodney had really followed Patsey about at Christmas ; no, that was not the right word, Rodney was a bit too stately and too busy to be a follower, but he had been attentive enough in the name of goodness! And she had asked Patsey rather than any of Patsey's cousins to come on this expedition because she was able quite naturally to let their movements be known to Rodney, and she rather expected he would stay at Lucerne on his return journey if he knew they were there. It all sounds very Victorian, but what could an aunt do at any date for an orphan niece to whom she wished well? And now Castle had come to Lucerne and had cut them dead!

She had thought Castle to be quite a man of the world until that moment, but anything less like a man of the world than to stare deliberately in at the window while pretending not to see them could not be imagined. Lady Lavington had put aside much that she cherished during the war, just as she had worn clothes out of fashion and had carried her own parcels. But now she had resumed her former standards of judgment with all the more zeal. She could not tolerate a boor, and a boor well born and well educated was inexcusable. Only a nasty temper or too much to drink could account for his appearance that evening. She hoped Patsey had seen him—he had looked so queer, it was the best cure. She was going by what the other cousins had said when she supposed that Patsey needed curing. She always believed in the opinion of contemporaries, or rather she disbelieved so much in the opinions of old people concerning the young that she was too easily swayed by the opinions of the young about each other.

" Has Patsey said anything ? " she had asked.

" Heavens, no, Aunt Mary ! Could you imagine Patsey saying anything ? "

" Then what did she do ? "

" Oh, she told several lies and that's new for Patsey."

And nothing more precise had been forthcoming, but somehow Lady Lavington had been convinced at the time and now she was annoyed.

" Well, it's to be hoped," she said, slipping the black lace gown from her beautiful shoulders, " that he won't try to make believe it didn't happen. I considered him to have rather particularly good manners, and I generally know."

And then, with a little shrug : " Even I am not infallible ! "

CHAPTER II

Seeking for Gemma

Next morning Rodney rose up a sane man but furious with himself. His first thought was of his rudeness to Lady Lavington. A little consideration made him decide that no direct apology was possible, and it was impossible to call without one. So, after tearing up several attempts, he wrote a note saying that he would leave it if he were unlucky in not finding them in. Then he watched from a safe vantage near the hotel until they had gone out in a motor—and left the note and his card with the porter.

" I hope," was the phrase he had chosen, " that you did not see a disreputable traveller pass under your window last night while you were at dinner. He was not fit to be recognised."

All the short morning before *déjeuner* he told himself that he was worrying about the brick he had dropped last night, and fearing that he might only get snubbed for his note to-day. That was why he could not enjoy himself, could not start on a long walk in that most delicious atmosphere. He was too restless and unsettled. Then after a brief meal, not noticing what he ate, he dropped the pretence that he was thinking about the Lavingtons. He

70

knew that the real thing he was aiming at was to call at Gemma's Pension at an hour at which she must be in, a thing impossible to make sure of. A waiter bringing his coffee to the lounge was surprised to see him leaving the hotel.

This time he took cover under the long alleys of clipped trees, so that he was invisible from the Schweitzerhof. As he walked very quickly in the direction of the little water railway, while crossing the river by the old wooden bridge of the " Dance of Death," it suddenly struck him that while he knew that Gemma was her name, and that she was Don Clemente's sister, he did not know her married name. It seemed to be the quaint custom in Lenno and Campo to call her always " Signora Gemma." It is awkward to call at a hotel and ask for a lady without mentioning her name. By the time the little train had taken him up into the pinewoods he had decided that he had something belonging to the Italian lady who had arrived from Chiasso last night—and a large tip might assist matters.

It was clear when he got into the pinewoods that this was the stopping place for further preparations. He walked up and down the broad brown path covered in by the branches so high above him, and there he tried to be calm and sensible.

The sweet mountain air, so light and gay after the rich heated atmosphere of the Italian lake country, was soothing. There is some reason other than racial why the Swiss look like their own cheerful toys, there is a commonsense in the air of Lucerne which should be infectious. Yet after a few moments he lost hold on to-day's sanity, for he could find no mental preparation for seeing Gemma. If he had longed to see her less or found it possible to believe in her, without a shadow of doubt he would not have felt this extraordinary trouble. In all his life of thirty-five years he had never been so distraught. Yesterday he had shared with her such austere noble thoughts, he had had glimpses of a soul more mystical and purified than any known to him. And then he had seen her accepting a secret communication from the scum of the earth, taking it on the sly, putting her hand in reach of it while her face looked past the man as if she did not know him. Rodney thereupon had seen red, until in a sudden reaction his farewell look had humbly asked pardon not without tears.

It was preposterous to have judged and condemned her for that unexplained action, but what had he in testimony on her side but just her powers of conversation in the train ? He had not seen her, had barely heard her mentioned forty-eight hours ago, why should he believe in her ? She had once been a Communist by her own confession, she had had difficulty in getting out of Italy perhaps for very good reasons from the point of view of wise government. But it was no use even attempting to test such thoughts to see if they held any sense, he despised them too much. No, there was something else, there was some claim on her perhaps, of personal kindness or charity—and then that seemed a poor explanation.

Indeed it is hard for passion not to be suspicious

even when it is not jealous. He could not feel that the secret acceptance of a letter from that Russian skunk was merely a charitable action !

Suddenly, before he had decided whether he would or would not ask her what were her relations with that noxious animal, and in what bonds her past political life had left her, he turned back from the broad path leading to Sonnenberg and hastened towards the Pension. It was impossible to miss the gaily painted board with the hand pointing to the little gate through which he had seen Gemma pass last night. He unlatched the gate and followed the path through the shrubbery. He was not in a mood for much observation, but as he came in sight of the hotel he had a vague impression that the building badly needed painting and the garden wanted attention. Then the huge dog he had heard baying last night seemed about to attack him and was called to order by the man who had taken Gemma's luggage and was now cutting some wood.

Rodney passed on towards what appeared to be the front door of the plain square building. The Pension faced the whole vast range of mountains to the south of the lake, while Lucerne lay immediately below. William Tell's chapel was one of the many little promontories that jutted out into the lake as it receded into the distance on the east. In the hard mid-day light the view looked too like all the dreadful oil paintings of the scene that were on sale in the town. But Rodney only wondered if Gemma were there and could see him from one of the many-

73

shuttered French windows. He pulled a bell-handle but no sound followed ; he looked in at the open door of the hall and had his first surprise in seeing that it was unfurnished, not a chair or a table or a mat was in it.

Could he have made a mistake, was the real Pension farther in the woods ? But when he stepped back he saw in huge gilt lettering the name of the Pension Victoria. On either side of the empty room which should have been a hall or lounge were two large rooms also unfurnished, except that one of them held a long deal table on trestles covered with lamps and clothing and piles of bottles and shoes, which in their disorder recalled to his mind the preparations for a jumble sale in the Parish Room when he was a child. In this room, apparently half asleep, was an untidy woman in a dirty white blouse and a shabby skirt ; he noticed her short fuzzy hair and her wide mouth. On seeing him, without apparently trying to wake up, she rose, opened the window and asked him what he wanted in a toneless voice in French. The weakness of his explanation, his ill-concealed eagerness and even his piece of Swiss gold did not disturb the weird effect of somnambulism. She answered in English—a poor compliment to Rodney's French :

"I will go look," and turned away and slowly went out of the room. Rodney Castle began to feel that he had probably made a hopeless mistake in coming here uninvited, but the idea that Gemma might appear at any moment was after all what mattered. Absorbed in watching the door through which the sleeping lady had disappeared, he was startled at a voice behind him. Turning round he saw a pale thin young man who (as he afterwards decided) was a degenerate, who might belong to any country, but who at any rate was awake.

" You ask for me ? "

Castle repeated his enquiries.

" It is a mistake, we have no visitors before August, no one has come here, the hotel is not open."

It seemed to Castle that he did not take the trouble to pretend to speak the truth, and his voice was almost as toneless as the woman's. Castle then explained quietly in French, as if the man had not understood his English, that he had himself come with the lady to the little gate where the gardener had taken her luggage.

The man said : " I will ask the gardener," and he walked off in the direction whence came the sounds of chopping wood. He was not away for two minutes and returned to Castle shrugging his shoulders.

" All a mistake ; the gardener did not understand, so took her luggage. When she find this hotel not open she went away ; probably she is in Lucerne, or she may have gone on to Sonnenberg. She left no address."

CHAPTER III

Fascists at the Villa Temple

"Villa Temple, Como.

" Dear Castle,—

"After the weeks you spent here and my enjoyment of your company I am sorry to have to tell you that you have left me in a pretty predicament! For the first time for forty years I am the object of suspicion to the local authorities—for such the Fascisti undoubtedly have become. It has needed tact and care on my part all these years, but I have up to now succeeded in keeping a quiet little position of my own and have been respected accordingly.

"The day after you left me, on coming in from a row on the lake, I found a tall young blackshirt in the hall examining my pictures of Mussolini. He looked charming but he was very stiff with me. He would not say one word beyond the business he had come on, and which amazed me.

"He wanted to know why I had arranged for a friend of mine to take Don Clemente's sister into Switzerland without a passport. I denied it utterly, and what was my annoyance when I found that he had proof that you had taken her to Chiasso in the motor I had got for you from Tommaso, and that you had been seen hurrying her through the barrier in spite of Tommaso's loud protests. He then in a few brief stern words gave me to understand that the lady has had a great and dangerous influence in this part of the country, and that while pretending to be a devout Catholic and a follower of Don Sturzo she is in reality a secret agent of the Bolsheviks.

" Now I know how all men, and Italians in particular, tell lies, and therefore if you can disprove these statements I shall be obliged. I said I had seen the lady sitting by the roadside, that you had thought she was in a difficulty, and that I had told you I did not know her so could not enquire what was the matter. As I talked he looked like a young crusader carved in black marble with an alabaster face, only I don't think any crusader's hair grew up into the air as if it were self-supporting. Anyhow, his face was quite impassive.

" It was a little hard for a devoted admirer of Fascism to see that all expressions of a fellow-feeling of admiration for Mussolini were taken to be a cowardly wish to be on the winning side, but so it was. You have noticed how my hand shakes (too much smoking I fear)—well, I could see he noticed that in an annoying way. He declined wine with a gesture suitable to a John the Baptist, and after giving the Fascist salute to the pictures of Mussolini went out clattering down the stone steps to his boat in which were two other blackshirts. They all three looked about my toy harbour as if it were large enough to contain an enemy fleet.

" I have been very much upset. I had welcomed
the new régime of law and order thinking that an old
man like myself could end his days here in peace.
However !

" Expecting to catch you at Lucerne and hoping
for an immediate reply,

" I am yours (and the next word was an indecipher-
able trail of the pen),

" ARTHUR TEMPLE."

It was cruelly unsympathetic towards his late kind
host, but Castle read the letter twice with no other
idea than the hope of finding in it the real name of
Don Clemente's sister. After that disappointment
he came to the conclusion that Temple was in a silly
old man's fuss. Last of all he faced the Fascist
accusation against Gemma, and to face it squarely
he went out at the back of the hotel and started for
a walk. The hotel stood to the east of the Hofkirche
and he turned that way, passed into the walled
churchyard and emerged again on the narrow steep
little road that rises to the Franciscan chapel near
the Drei Linden.

His annoyance at the letter he had just received
grew at every step. But the queer element of cruel
suspicion, so characteristic of passion as contrasted
with the greater human affections, had gone. And
this letter with its false accusations roused all his
capacity for championship. He had reached the
fourth faded little fresco of the *Way of the Cross* in
that path that forty years ago was so immensely

charming and is so no longer. But though the most hideous villas now spoil the old charm there is still the wide view of the town. He had turned absently looking down without interest on the sharp spires of the Hofkirche rising like black needles that are so insistently mediæval amid all the horrors of successful hotel life.

He took Temple's letter out of his pocket and read it again. Would it be any use at all to ask the old person what was the name of the lady thus accused ? How could he frame a letter of apology that might produce at least the name in reply ?

" Good morning."

It was Patsey Lavington's voice, cool and clear, and with just the tang of a reminder that he ought not to overlook her presence.

After he had caught off his cap and greeted her with eager politeness she laughed.

" Now that was quite all right and I can go on and leave you to finish reading your letter. I am going up to the Linden trees. Good-bye ! "

" Mayn't I come too ? " He really wanted to go with her.

She had taken two long steps above him and their eyes met on a level.

" It's not necessary, you know." Her grey eyes were laughing though her manner was very serious.

" How do you mean not necessary ? " He crushed the letter into his pocket and walked on with her.

" I mean that good manners do not really make

79

it necessary for you to go for a walk with me just because we chanced to meet this morning."

"Ah," he said, "I deserve that, and perhaps it is also a suggestion that you would rather I went back ? "

"On the contrary I was on the lookout for you." Her manner was extremely cool and business-like. "I want to tell you something that you ought to know."

Then she paused until he was by her side, when she walked on quickly with rather long steps. It occurred to Rodney that Patsey, who was kindness itself, wanted to make things right and really comfortable between Lady Lavington and himself. He waited.

"Aunt Mary has had a letter from her old friend Mr. Temple, and he is in quite a fuss," she paused. "Well, I think you know all about it, because you were reading a letter on his unmistakably beautiful notepaper."

Rodney gave a sharp sigh : " I only wish I did know all about it ! "

"Well," Patsey perhaps wanted to give him time, " Sir John and Aunt Mary think that it's either a pure invention, or that you did give the lady a lift and know no more about her. They are sure you would not have helped her to get away without a passport."

"But Gemma did have a passport," he burst out.

"Gemma ! what a fascinating name."

"I saw the passport official look at it and stamp

it, but I did not look at it myself. I wish to heaven I had—because then I should know her surname."

"Gemma, only Gemma," murmured Patsey.

"Then why did those people who wear black shirts, which must be dreadful in hot weather, why did they say she had gone without a passport ? "

"Why did they tell all the lies Temple puts in his letter to me, except that they want to ruin her or to hit at somebody else through her ? "

"Well, Sir John says that if her brother belongs to the Catholic democratic party, they are no more Red than English Liberals," said Patsey in her gentle cool voice.

"Exactly," said Castle fervently. And he proceeded in a sudden flow to present some of the features of Gemma's story to Patsey as Gemma had presented them to himself on that wonderful journey. As this went on they reached the Franciscan chapel, and passing beyond made their way through the fields up to the Drei Linden.

Patsey understood him perfectly, and thought it was all so like him, indeed so like a man. But Gemma seemed more mysterious ; it was easy to see what were Rodney's emotions, but the reflection of Gemma on such a troubled surface was indistinct. Patsey's manner to Rodney was kindness and sympathy itself, she felt for him very truly for his trouble was great, perhaps even greater than her own. Patsey always grasped a nettle if it stung her, a habit that accumulates strength even if it is not true that no power to sting remains.

" Did—did Gemma go on further when you got out at Lucerne ? Did you part from her that night ? "

" She got out at Lucerne, I did part from her that night, but I did not know what it meant," and then he told the rest, only suppressing the unpleasant Russian at the station.

" Good Heavens ! " Patsey cried. And as they reached the Linden trees she turned to a bench and sat down suddenly while he stood by her.

Gemma lost—just as she had faced up to this fact of Gemma, just as she had determined to be very good to Gemma, to be in it all and help Rodney, Gemma was lost ! She at once saw two alternatives, one that the blackshirt man was right—she was a ' Red ' spy, a traitor—and the other that she was in some personal danger, was the victim of some conspiracy. Then she shook her head and tried to regain commonsense.

" But why should you know where she is ? I think we are going daft both of us. You don't expect to follow up everyone you travel with surely. You don't know where all the other people in the train went to. Why shouldn't it be true that she made a mistake about the hotel, and that it was not open and she went on to another ? "

" If you had seen the man at the Pension you would have known he was lying. Besides—the hotel not open ! It's the end of June now, there's not a stick of furniture or a pot of paint ! Every other hotel in Lucerne is half full at least, and as spick and

span as if it were August. I've tried Cook and all
the agents and they won't talk about it, there's
something fishy. One man hinted to me that those
who will pry into other people's concerns are bound
to suffer for it."

Patsey pressed a thin hand on her forehead.
" Yes," she said, " I feel it in my bones. Though
you haven't anything like proof, you're right, they've
got hold of her. Rodney, we can't let it alone, we
must find Gemma."

How his face brightened ! It was not until later
on that he reflected that her ' we ' was a remarkable
gesture and that he had no right to accept it. He
sat down on the short grass at her feet and they
talked and talked but they seemed to get no for-
rarder. It was such a thin poor story and there was
no earthly reason why they should mix themselves
up in it. To Aunt Mary and to Sir John it would of
course be mischievous nonsense. It would be nonsense because they were not of the kind to expect
drama in life, and mischievous because although
great villains and dark plots were usually imagined
by the foolish it was mischievous to believe in them
—as such ideas threw young people into dangerous
company.

The rescue party first agreed that they might
involve Gemma in great danger if they approached
the police. To whom could they turn ? There were
English diplomatists at Berne, there was the Secretariat at Geneva. Then Patsey gave a desperate
laugh :

" Fancy any one of them all paying attention to such a story ! "

The longer they talked the more perplexed did they become. Lady Lavington received some very meagre information that afternoon.

" I met Rodney Castle, and it is all such nonsense, Aunt Mary. She had her passport all right and she hates the Reds. He is writing to Arthur Temple to say that he does not know where she is but they ought to get her address and let her defend herself. And he would like Temple to tell us what happens. Rodney will give evidence himself at any time. They might be examined together if she is in Switzerland."

" It's all very well," said Lady Lavington coldly, " but I am very sorry for Arthur Temple, and I think Mr. Castle might have been more considerate in return for the hospitality at the villa."

CHAPTER IV

ANOTHER FAILURE

IT was two days after Rodney's confidences to Patsey when she called him up.

" Are you quite sure it is you I am speaking to ? "

Rodney reassured her laughingly.

" Well I may be wrong but I think I have seen her. We are just starting for Sonnenberg, we are driving round to the funicular station opposite Mount Pilatus. I must not stop, but if you can come up there now, or look in here this evening, I'll explain."

Of course he started at once, called a taxi and was just going to tell the man to go to the further station when it occurred to him that he would go by the nearest funicular from which he would get into the Gütsch pinewoods and walk up to Sonnenberg from there. Of the two he thought he might be at the Sonnenberg before they were. He had been feeling desperately anxious and gloomy picturing every sort of horror for Gemma, even a forced journey to Russia, when Patsey had sent him this ray of hope. Now he looked about him with keen anxious eyes, he was engaged in that dreadful occupation of trying to see on all sides at once, to see into trains and motors and carriages without missing one figure on the pavement. It was possible to be constantly near each other and not know it—perhaps to know it just afterwards, always too late.

After the short drive in the heat the shadows of the trees inside the toy station were pleasant. There he had stood with Gemma that first evening wasting the precious moments in an idiotic fury of suspicion. He got into the little carriage and heard the water emptying itself. Oh if he could but have her by his side now in safety how he would explain!

His thoughts were so full of her that when the two carriages one going up and one down flashed past each other midway he almost missed the instantaneous vision of Gemma in which their eyes met as she passed him. The moment would have been too brief for a snapshot, it was as if he had received a pistol-shot rather than seen for a moment what he had longed for. Yet he thought he could have touched her, could have called her name had he only been less astonished to see her. And now he just kept himself in, he knew it was perfectly useless to do anything to stop the little train on its inevitable three or four minutes' journey. So he reached the top, took another ticket and came down again.

Would she wait for him? Surely she would, she could not do otherwise in common courtesy, for really he had done a good deal for her on that journey from Lenno. As he reached the platform at the foot of the hill there were five or six people waiting, but no Gemma—but on the other side of the turnstile—out in the street?

He knew it before he got sight of the pavement

and the houses and the people. He knew Gemma would not be there. He hurried along, caught up a taxi and pursued the distant tram, but he knew she would not be in it, and again he was right. Then he went to the railway station where he knew he would not find her, and to the little piers from which the steamers take the crowd out on the lake, where he knew she would not be. Then he remembered the organ recital at the Hofkirche, but he knew as he went in and before he could look round that Gemma was not in the audience. It seemed as if he had a knowledge of her absence before his senses showed him she was not there.

CHAPTER V

Patsey sees Gemma

Patsey did not betray that she was worried while having tea at Sonnenberg, but she was worried at Rodney not joining them. Aunt Mary and Sir John always talked well, but to-day whatever they talked about was not to the point. They walked slowly back through the woods down to Gütsch, stopping for moments of admiration or to rest on fallen trees. The elders enjoyed themselves in a gentle irresponsible way while Patsey felt the weight of international intrigues pressing on her young shoulders. She was sure that she had seen Gemma and that she had seen her in dangerous company. She had been out sketching that morning trying to get a bit of the old wall and its watch-tower for a foreground, and the spires of the Hofkirche sharp and black in the distance.

Then a little figure, a very small lame woman had come through the gateway in the old wall and had sat down by the roadside. This weird little figure reminded her of the strange specimens of humanity that Piranesi used to hide in corners of his amazing architectural dreams, the human beings that seemed to suggest that he had seen those magnificent masses of Roman remains in nightmares.

PATSEY SEES GEMMA

This little figure was terribly vital though deformed. Patsey felt her to be curiously malignant and dangerous. It wanted courage to turn over the pages of her sketch book and set to work at a portrait. Impossible ! What on earth was it that gave that impression of intellectual power, of adventure, of cruelty, not the impish cruelty of the small abnormal little beings male or female who, like insects, must make mischief of some sort ; this creature was small and abnormal in body no doubt but she was in some way big, capable, experienced and dangerous. Patsey was doing better than she knew, her black pencil gave an indication at least of what she felt about this extraordinary being.

And then another figure moved slowly into view through the archway and sat down by the little, deformed, half burnt out volcano of a woman whom Patsey was daring to sketch. The newcomer was seated before she drew Patsey's attention and then it was impossible not to study the contrast. This woman was as graceful as the other was deformed, her face as noble as the other's was ignoble for all its vitality and power. Her attitude, elbow on knee and her hand supporting her chin, woke some idea in Patsey's memory. The newcomer sat down on a big stone with a long cloak falling from her shoulders, the hat was quite hidden by the veil that fell into the straight folds of the cloak. Then she remembered that Rodney had told her how he had seen Gemma sitting in a long cloak on a big stone, and how Arthur Temple had declared that she looked as if she had come off the ceiling of the Sistine chapel. Of course that was Gemma and this was Gemma. But good Heavens in what company! Patsey now worked for all she was worth on another page of her book. This sketch was much harder than the other, and she was right this time in thinking that she was doing it badly. But she had the advantage with them both that they sat as still as if they wanted to help her. Then suddenly the deformity tried to raise itself and fell back. The other rose and looked down on her with tragic pity which the recipient of such tenderness furiously resented as it seemed to Patsey.

But the beautiful, the strong and noble figure gently raised the other, who accepted her service very haughtily and they disappeared through the archway together.

" The little monster looks as if she thinks she is the master," thought Patsey as her unconscious models left her.

That afternoon Patsey found it hard to behave as if nothing had happened and to be pleasant and say bright things while her imagination was obsessed by what she had seen. It is a mistake to suppose that the modern girl who drives a motor and knows all about everything and likes to have a hand in everything practical has got rid of imagination. Very often the imagination is more strained and burdened in the present order of things than in the old. Fifty years ago Patsey's imagination might have devoured itself feeding on her own sorrows, weeping over disappointed hopes, watching the canker working in her heart. Now she was distracted from the sorrow of it by absorption in the drama of life. And with this came that terrible youthful taking on of responsibility, that sense of having to help and of self-blame if things go wrong. Sir John, who had held high and responsible positions; Lady Lavington, a grandmother and the centre of many circles, had no such overpowering sense of responsibility as Patsey had. It needs time and experience to know the narrow limits within which good can be done and evil averted, so that there results the inclination to leave most things alone.

When the Lavingtons and Sir John came out of the Schweizerhof after dinner they found Castle waiting for them under the bleached alley of lime trees by the water. The elders sat down, and Rodney and Patsey walked quickly away from them.

There was an air of haste and of importance about them which impressed the two left on the bench not unfavourably.

Patsey held out her sketch book—" Well ? "

He caught at it. " Yes, yes, no doubt of it. That's Gemma."

" But turn back a page, that is the woman she was with, only she was far, far more horrible than that."

Rodney's face took on a grey hue.

" I wish," said Patsey, " I could have caught Gemma when she bent over to help the little monster. A guardian angel—only I don't believe angels are wasted on the care of devils ! "

" But what conceivably can it mean ? " And then he explained what had prevented his coming to Sonnenberg in the afternoon—the vision for a second and the long futile hunt afterwards.

" Do you know," said Patsey, " I believe the person you ought to find is Don Clemente. Supposing they have got some hold on Gemma he is surely the one to get at her."

" I am trying to get at him. I have asked a friend of mine who is in London, a Roman Catholic, to see what he can do. I suggested the Italian Church as a place where they might know of Don Clemente. I asked for a telegram if he could give me the address and it might come at any moment now. But if that fails I am at my wits' ends ! "

" Somehow we must find him. If this fails, one of us must go to Geneva, everybody is known to some-one in Geneva."

" I wonder if it would be of any use to consult Sir John ? "

" Oh no ! " cried Patsey in horrified unbelief of any utility in the old. " Fancy what it would sound like to him ! You help a woman to get over the frontier, she then confides to you her life story. Arthur Temple reports that she is a Bolshevik. You and I have seen her in the queerest company, and yet we ask a British general to help us to rescue her from the Bolshies because we choose to disbelieve Arthur Temple's report. He would think the story a bit thin ! "

PATSEY SEES GEMMA

" But is there anybody in Geneva who would believe it either ? "

" No, only Don Clemente would believe us and so we *must* find him, and Geneva seems the most promising place to go to."

" You are wonderful ! "

Patsey was startled at finding that his attention was diverted to herself. She blushed, she found the compliment rather painful.

" Wonderful to think of Geneva ! " She turned to him laughing.

" No, wonderful to believe so firmly in Gemma."

" I've seen her," said Patsey shortly.

" But you believed in her before yesterday, before you had seen her."

" I caught it from you I suppose." Patsey's voice had a little shake, a little trill up to a high note.

" It is splendid of you ! "

It was much more splendid than he knew, this faith kindled by his faith.

They had walked away from the hotels and were standing looking out on the water. If there had been no Gemma ! If Patsey had wished for more knowledge of life she was certainly getting it, but in the wonders of that June night it was not knowledge she wanted, for the mind does not warm the heart whereas the heart can really warm the mind. The moon was cold on the snows of the Alps of the Oberland and the Unterwalden, and the electric light was hard in the town behind them.

" Life is very sad," said Patsey.

93

THE SHADOW OF MUSSOLINI

" Very sad," said Rodney.

They were both bearing a burden, both longed for relief, both felt a pain that for want of experience they called intolerable. And all they could say was this little comment on life that it was very sad.

Whereas if it had not been for Gemma they might have stood there together full of life and glorying in it. They would not have used many words but their eyes would have said to each other : " You know all about it as well as I do." That is the pride of that joy in the conquest of each other. For each knows life and that it is good on the supreme testimony of the other. Theirs was now the commonest trouble in the world, so common that it is hard for the lookers on not to get blunted to the tragedy. It is often caused, as in this case, by what seems the purely chance entry of the destructive element. Rodney had given Gemma a lift and that was why he and Patsey felt very lonely on that warm and beautiful night in June.

Lady Lavington and Sir John meanwhile had the pleasant feeling of marking time in delightful conditions while the young enjoyed themselves. And to them was added another friend belonging to their world. Lady Lavington saw the neat figure of Arthur Temple coming along the green alley with pleasure, she knew so well the gift the little man had for good company when with the people he liked.

PATSEY SEES GEMMA

He would be a great addition in these pleasant lazy days. And he began, as indeed she expected him to go on, asking her news of the friends they shared, giving just the effect of domestic intimacy with people worth knowing.

But this nice little pastime was interrupted by Temple himself. He gave a sharp sigh.

"The truth is that I am coming away from the Villa Temple sooner than I had meant to and I shall be in London earlier than I wished. It is best to get into touch with the Italian ambassador as soon as I can. I can convince him that I am a keen, a devoted Fascist. Is Castle still in Lucerne?"

"He is here somewhere about walking with Patsey."

"Well I can only say I hope he's ashamed of himself."

"I think he is. There was certainly something wrong with him when he got here."

"Dons are so tiresome," grumbled Temple, "too simple and confiding, as if the whole world were a large Oxford."

Lady Lavington forbore to remind him that Castle had seen a good deal of a world very unlike Oxford during the war. She adroitly asked him why he believed in the Fascists and he got going at a quick pace and presently both listeners were absorbed. One thing that cannot be said of Mussolini is that his name is a drag on conversation. He had become an obsession to the little old gentleman as to many others of his fellow mortals, so that Temple was really upset at his present "false position," as he called it, for which he had only Rodney to blame. This trouble was partly purely sentimental and greatly an acute fear of annoyance where he had looked for more peace and stability in his old age.

As he would hark back to Castle's conduct, Lady Lavington ventured to say that surely it made a great difference to the story that, as Patsey declared, the lady had had a passport.

" Yes, but he knew perfectly well that nobody else would take her to the frontier. Tommaso says they were in a nice fright when they got near Chiasso ! And now he has the impertinence to try to follow her up through me ! Through me ! " He raised his little shaky hands in protest. " As if he hadn't done enough mischief already ! He thinks he has done it so cleverly that I cannot read between the lines, but I can. I can. I wish I had never had the fellow to stay with me. He will get into some scrape. My dear lady, I wonder if you are wise in letting him go about with your delightful Patsey ? He may be hunting for this woman among the Bolsheviks that are all over Switzerland intriguing to get back into Italy. "

Lady Lavington tried not to laugh, but Sir John to her surprise cross-questioned Arthur Temple very minutely.

" I can't see," the General concluded, with an air of kindly authority, " that Castle has done more than wish to clear himself."

PATSEY SEES GEMMA

" But he wants to know her name ? " fumed Temple.

Sir John smiled but did not answer, for the culprit came upon them suddenly from among the trees with Patsey. Great was the warmth of Arthur Temple's greeting to the young lady and equally warm was her greeting of him—very coldly he told Castle that they must have a talk next day.

" He is cultivating a Fascist manner," whispered Castle to Patsey, as they all moved forward to the Schweizerhof.

Lady Lavington found it hard not to laugh at Temple's warning as to the danger of Patsey going about Lucerne with Rodney Castle. It seemed so absurd to suppose that her niece and a highly respectable Oxford don could run any risk of coming across live Bolsheviks. Her imagination was not equal to the suggestion. She thought it was all some stupid mistake about the lady Rodney had met on the journey, and she did not for a moment believe she was a Bolshevik. She might have been an attraction without being a Bolshevik, but clearly Castle's devotion to her niece was even more than it had been in London in the winter, and she was not afraid that the lady of the frontier adventure could be a rival. Even the morning after his arrival Rodney's note of apology had made Lady Lavington feel that she had made too much of a momentary lapse, and by now her good opinion of him was entirely restored.

She cordially agreed, two days after Temple's arrival, to Patsey going on an expedition alone with

G

Rodney to Basel, starting early and returning late. Writing to one of the other nieces that day, she mentioned that Patsey was out for the day with Rodney with satisfaction, knowing that the bit of news would not be overlooked.

The object of the expedition was to see a friend of Don Clemente, for all the information Rodney had received from London was the address of a man who might know where he was, a Frenchman, M. Evriat, living in Basel. Patsey suggested going herself because she could not stand a whole day of Arthur Temple's patter and the slow walks of the elders. Besides, they had not really had time to discuss what to do next if they could not find Don Clemente.

CHAPTER VI

THE DEATH IN THE TRAIN

IT was an irritated and slightly shamefaced Rodney
after Temple's dressing down had been administered,
for though not ashamed of what he had done, he
was a little ashamed of his own indifference to
Temple's real or fancied trouble.

Patsey's company and the beauty of the day and
the glory of the world were all cheering, and it was
an unconscious relief to leave Lucerne and the
unending futile scrutiny of the passers-by behind.

When they got to Basel, Patsey made her way to
the Cathedral while Rodney went to ask for M.
Evriat. He found the house, an attractive old
building with a large shady garden, but the master
was out, and the old servant had no idea when he
would be back.

During the day, at intervals of about an hour, he
tried again until the maid got fairly sick of the sight
of him. Between whiles there were meals and a visit
to the Cathedral, but on the whole it was a futile
sort of day. After tea Patsey suggested that she
should go home alone and Rodney stay the night,
but that plan he did not think would be approved of
by Lady Lavington and he refused to let her go
alone. So he wrote a long letter in the hotel near

the Cathedral and left it at M. Evriat's house. Then by a mistake he went back to the hotel whereas Patsey was waiting for him outside the station. It ended in Patsey nearly missing the train to Lucerne and Rodney quite missing it. The manner of this accident was part of what seemed to Rodney the dreadful chain of coincidences in which he had been caught. For just as they hurried on to the platform he was almost sure that he saw Gemma standing by some luggage that was being put on the train. He called to Patsey not to wait, he would only be a moment. He had not intended to desert Patsey, but when she looked out of the carriage window to look for him the train moved off and she saw him run forward just too late.

At the moment she had a feeling of horror of being deserted quite new to her, for what was this little journey compared to others she had done alone? She stood at the window feeling as if she could not turn round, could not face the compartment behind her. As she jumped in she had seen that it was almost empty—only one seat occupied. But this was absurd and Patsey sat down in the seat by the window facing the engine. She was also facing, though not exactly opposite, her fellow passenger—
" Oh," the word escaped her before she could cover her mouth with her handkerchief. What was opposite was the horrible thing she had seen and sketched two days ago.

Patsey leant towards the open window for breath, and then having gained a measure of self-

command she began stealthily to examine the
creature and saw that its eyes were shut. It was
worse than she remembered. It was hunchbacked
and crooked and, sitting as it did now, it looked like
a mechanical figure of which the springs were broken.
The clothes on it were of faded magnificence—was
it moving ? Patsey turned her eyes to look up at
the stars and then ventured to scrutinise again. Yes,
silks and sables and pearls. Heavens what pearls !
And the dirty misshapen little fingers wore gorgeous
gems. Had the monster been to some monstrous
social gathering ? Patsey had plenty of pluck, but
the woman made her feel sorely sick and afraid.
They were in a first-class carriage and she had the
impression that the train was very empty. She
could easily move into another compartment if she
could pass the thing on the opposite side. She got
up and moved very quietly, but as she was reaching
the door, with eyes carefully averted from the seated
figure, a voice said in French :

" Gemma, Gemma don't go, don't leave me alone."

Patsey stood with her hand on the door. The
wretched creature must be blind, so she could safely
escape. Then she looked down and met large eyes
like exhausted volcanoes that clearly were not blind,
nor could they see rightly.

" Gemma the drops in the bag, in mercy." Hard
quick breathing was audible. Patsey did not hesitate
now. She looked for the bag, an old morocco case,
which she lifted on to the seat and opened. Amidst
gorgeous jewelled fittings was a little bottle, a drop

measure and a medicine glass. On the bottle was
written something she could not read.

" Quick, ten drops ! "

It was not easy to measure exactly in a shaking
train, but clearly there was no time to lose. She held
the glass to the dreadful mouth, for even in the
moment of compassion—and Patsey was com-
passionate—she could not feel an iota less of repulsion.

" You are very ill."

" How clever to discover that ! What an idiot
you are. I may be dead in five minutes or I may
not. Anyhow I am not going to make dying speeches,
every paper in Europe would report them if I did."
Getting accustomed to the tormented face, Patsey
saw written on it a monstrous vanity and self-
complacence.

" I will tell you only two things."

" But I'm not Gemma."

Was she mad or drunk or delirious that she would
not or could not understand ? The eyes were getting
stranger. Patsey made a supreme effort and felt
her pulse, at which she was horrified.

" I must get somebody. I must call the guard."
She pressed the bell and opened the door and called,
but her voice sounded like a whisper in the noise of
the train. She was hesitating whether to leave the
poor woman alone while she rushed for help, when
she felt her wrist caught in a close grip from which
there seemed no escape.

" Gemma kill or be killed—remember——"

Why had she not torn herself away, was a question

that worried Patsey afterwards. Partly, no doubt, it was because it seemed impossible to use force, partly because she could still press the bell with her right hand and still hoped it might be heard, but also Patsey in the horror of her position lost her judgment and it was all over before she recovered herself.

" I am not Gemma," she protested. " Let me go for a doctor."

" Not Gemma, not Gemma," moaned the woman, but she did not release her hold. The eyes closed for a moment and reopened in a state of pure delirium, exultant and crazy. Something Patsey thought she understood, some babbling of crown jewels and state motors, some glorying of a horrid kind. Then in a faint voice, in great scorn, were some words no longer in French but in Italian, evidently with an effort at distinct pronunciation :

" Ah piccolino Benito Mussolini traditore, nessuna pietà ! Gemma, Gemma ! "

An indescribable change passed over the face as the spirit made its flitting.

Patsey's wrist was still in the grip of the dead hand when the ticket collector found them alone together.

CHAPTER VII

FIRST AID FOR THE DEAD

RODNEY had missed the train and had also missed Gemma, if indeed she had really been there to miss. Of course it was not extraordinary to lose sight of her in a crowded station with many exits, it was certainly no proof that she had not been there. But he knew that in his present obsession every long cloak and veil seemed to him to conceal Gemma. Once he had followed a nun out of the station at Lucerne under this delusion.

About half an hour after the train had taken Patsey out of sight, he remembered to telephone to the Schweizerhof to say that she would arrive alone and had better be met—a communication to which Sir John answered with a grunt that would have terrified any member of his staff in days past. The next train was the express from Paris to Milan and would not arrive at Lucerne till six in the morning. It was now ten o'clock and Rodney decided to make another attempt to see the friend of Don Clemente.

He got to the old house as the Cathedral clock struck the quarter. The door was opened by a very large priest, who asked him in Italian to turn into a room on the right. The room was sparely furnished with some admirable old things, carved and inlaid, while one or two finely toned pictures met his eyes.

" I came to ask," said Rodney in French, " if you could give me the address of Don Clemente."

The large priest was now seated. He seemed to Rodney a fine specimen of the Northern Italian, almost burly, who must have been handsome before he grew stout.

" What do you want it for ? Do you know him ?" Even those few words betrayed that his French was as ugly as his voice was beautiful. The manner was direct and open. Clearly he meant to know more before he answered the stranger's question.

" You are his friend and therefore I will tell you." Rodney hesitated, the other watched him, openly taking stock of his manner and hesitations.

" Do you know him well ? " Rodney asked.

The priest took a large pinch of snuff and smiled : " Not as well as I ought to, no doubt, but I have had his acquaintance all my life."

Even while wondering whether to make the plunge, Rodney was not too pre-occupied to feel admiration of the voice, for he had never heard so much tone indicating such reserves of strength in any voice as in this one. Rodney looked at him again, the strong electric light made the big head, the black hair and the olive skin imposing in its vitality against the black oak that was its background. He did not feel certain whether he liked him or not, whether he should decide to trust him

or not, partly of course because the man clearly mis-
trusted his nocturnal visitor.

"Whatever you can tell Clemente, you can tell
me," he flung out carelessly enough.

"It is about his sister."

"Ah!" The face changed completely, the mobile
features expressed an unconcealed anxiety. "I am
Clemente," he said. "M. Evriat is out. About my
sister, speak s'il vous plaît."

While Rodney told the little he had to say, the
listener's face showed an astonishing range of
emotion. He made an occasional large and expressive
gesture, but he did not speak. Rodney suppressed
nothing, neither the disgusting Russian at the
station, nor Patsey's report of the monstrous little
woman. For both of these Don Clemente could, if
he had chosen, have supplied a name. The end of
Rodney's story brought him to his supposed glimpse
of Gemma an hour ago. "Gemma did not leave
then by the late train. She must be in Basel, but
Heaven only knows where!"

"You knew she was here!" enquired Rodney.

"I knew she had been here. When I arrived this
evening she left me a letter, but she only said that she
was leaving by the last train. You looked every way?
And the Russian and that woman, did you see either
of them to-night too?"

No, he had thought Gemma was alone.

The ice was broken. Don Clemente burst into
Italian and spoke quicker and quicker. Yet each
word—there was soon a record number of words to

the minute—was absolutely distinct and the voice seemed to gain rather than lose in impressiveness.

He followed Rodney's dates in his story and supplemented his facts. He said he had left Gemma at Campo because he had to hurry through to Paris to make his preparations for his approaching journey to Africa. An old cousin had been due to arrive just after he had left. He had told Gemma to telegraph as soon as she arrived at Lucerne. It was arranged that she should stay at the old-fashioned Pension with her cousin. He had received a telegram from Lucerne on the day expected with no address, and one brief letter followed saying that she was very well and resting ; she was not at the Pension, as it did not open till August. She had begged him not to write, and above all not to give his address.

" Knowing Gemma," her brother continued, " I was alarmed and came off here at once. Her plans and plots are of a simplicity ! Fancy thinking that this letter would reassure me. Some day her care for me will land her God knows where ! But now ! " And then he rapidly reviewed the situation. " Who can look after Gemma," he said, " without increasing her present danger ? I have engaged myself definitely for the foreign missions and must sail within a month."

He knew, he declared, that she must have some wild plan for the good of her people. " No one knows better than Gemma that for me, a Catholic Liberal, to be associated with Bolsheviks would be ruin, and

not to myself alone but to my party—ruin at the
Vatican, ruin with the Fascists, seizing as they do
every imaginary charge against me. In Italy you do
not associate with the people with whom you disagree,
even if they are respectable, and for Gemma to be
seen with this scum of Hell! She would know the
dangers thoroughly. They have got her in their
toils by some threat at me. They hate us Christian
liberals because we save the souls of the people, and
each soul we save or make Christian becomes something they cannot reach, cannot possess. They covet
to possess souls even as we would give them to
Christ. Gemma," he suddenly spoke very slowly,
" Gemma has one passion, one ambition—to bring
souls to Christ."

The face, more strong and vital than spiritual in
its usual aspect, was suddenly aglow from some
light within. He was unconscious of the Englishman
for the moment. From the moment he had decided
to trust Rodney, he seemed to lose all inclination to
scrutiny or criticism, and at moments forgot all
about him. Any Frenchman would have remembered, with or without sympathy, that Rodney was
a youngish man and Gemma a young woman. But
in fact Clemente was accustomed to modern ways
and to Gemma's admirers, who were rarely so trouble-
some as to become lovers. She saw to it that they
were too busy working for her ideals. He saw her
too always as Cæsare's widow.

The door opened in that moment of silence, and
a little man, small, spare and neat, came in quickly.

FIRST AID FOR THE DEAD

He gave a piece of paper to Don Clemente. The latter glanced at it and rose.

" This is le M. Evriat with whom I am staying, for whom you are asking. You will excuse me."

The little Frenchman looked all the smaller for replacing Don Clemente in the great oak chair. He inquired courteously what Rodney wanted, and his voice sounded thin and metallic.

" I have had more than I asked for. I came here at the suggestion of a friend of yours in London, to ask you for Don Clemente's address, and found I was speaking to himself."

" You knew him already ? "

" No."

" Perhaps you know relations or friends of his ? "

" I have met his sister."

M. Evriat gave a gesture that seemed to say, " Oh well, that explains everything."

" You are interested in Italian affairs—you were there in the war perhaps ? "

" I was not. I fought on the French front and hardly took in how greatly they were suffering in Italy."

The Frenchman shrugged his shoulders. " Every nation suffered, but some exaggerate. There is one nation that cannot exaggerate—she suffered too much."

Rodney felt irritated by the last remark.

" I have been interested in Italian politics during the last few weeks."

" Mussolini is a great man."

THE SHADOW OF MUSSOLINI

" Yes, but——"

" Mussolini is a very great man," Evriat went on. ' But me no buts ' was expressed in the wave of his hand. " To oppose him is pure folly—it is to oppose the interests of Italy, of the church, of Europe. These good people——" he shrugged his thin little shoulders again. " But see, he has defeated the Freemasons, he has put the crucifix back in the schools. I do not say he is a believer, a *dévot*, but what can they get ? Moonshine, fantastic dreams of liberty. They can't get Manzoni out of their poor heads ! What is the use of being free to send anybody you like to sit in the Chamber, of writing any sedition you like, of refusing to work as much as you like, if you are not able to get food, or wholesome conditions of life ? That nineteenth century craze for one sort of liberty for men and women, what slavery it has led to ! Slavery to hunger, to fear of violence, to the laws of nature that won't be trifled with. These good people of the Partito Popolare with their fidelity to old shibboleths ! And the women of course are the worst dreamers of all. They will do most of the mischief. See just now, if they upset Mussolini, what have they got in his place ? They know they can't replace him. The men would be sensible and wait, but I don't trust a woman, if she gets this craze for the mechanism of government. Women adore the machine, because it used to be a toy kept out of their reach, and when it does not function they cannot see that the system is worn out—they put more weight on the weakest link in the chain ! "

FIRST AID FOR THE DEAD

Rodney was getting restless. It seemed absurd for him to take up arms on behalf of the Partito Popolare, but the little man who was so keen to dissociate himself from his friend Don Clemente did not attract him. He would have gone away, only he was hoping to see the Italian again.

"Mind you," said the Frenchman in a low voice, "as you meet them here, I feel bound to warn you. Trust Don Clemente as much as you like, but believe me, his sister, whose husband was a furious Socialist, though she began with noble intentions, is certainly in with the Reds. He won't believe it, but there are proofs. She has had too much influence. She thought she could pull all the strings. She wanted to show the Bolsheviks that you could be a Socialist and a Christian at the same time."

Rodney let him finish, let him run down naturally before he seized on one word he had spoken.

"Meet her here ? Will she be here ? "

"Here ? She is upstairs at this moment with her brother, or was so five minutes ago."

Rodney at those words felt for the first time that it was possible to think of Gemma with joy, not merely with anxiety and strain and longing. Such a peaceful delight entered into his whole being at the news that she was under the same roof. He had not really owned to himself before that he was her very humble lover. He had deceived himself by the make-believe that he was only anxious for her safety. He sat forward a little that his cheerful countenance might not be read too easily.

THE SHADOW OF MUSSOLINI

" Ah ! " said M. Evriat, " he is calling me." And he hurried out of the room, shutting the door after him. But he reopened it instantly.

" He asks you to come upstairs."

The little man with several bows opened the door into a long low room, lit with shaded lamps. Rodney might have been dazzled by a thousand lights for all he saw of the room after he had seen that it was empty of Gemma. Don Clemente was standing by the window, just betraying that his calmness was the result of an effort, his immobility the effect of training.

" I must apologise for leaving you so abruptly, but my sister came here. We must have a little council of three." He smiled with an effort. " M. Evriat, may I explain the meeting to itself ? "

They sat down, Rodney facing Evriat and the priest across a blackened refectory table loaded with books and papers.

" M. Evriat is a distinguished French Catholic publicist, who would be known to you if you lived in any other university than Oxford or perhaps Cambridge. He is violently pro-Mussolini, and would tell you that as a looker-on he knows more of the game, as you say in England, than I do. In short we differ profoundly except on religion and mutual esteem." Evriat noted that Don Clemente was gaining time, for what purpose he was not clear. " Now you are an Englishman, a modernist in religion, interested in the problems of to-day to the extent of wishing to benefit the working classes, but

much preferring to study the classics and to play
something—probably golf."

Rodney only half took in what the voice was
saying, but its restrained force and natural sympathy
helped him. He was looking at the big man hungrily
though he did not know it. He wanted help and
while Clemente spoke he was getting it.

"But my friend M. Evriat and I are united in a
common object and he believes in my sincerity," he
laughed, "partly because my interests are deeply
engaged on his side for the moment. Well, to come
to the point. M. Evriat returned to his maternal
home at Berne because he had reason to think that
the life of his hero Mussolini was in danger from the
Bolsheviks' plots. He wished to get to them in their
own nests. I asked M. Evriat to let me come here
because I had good reason to think that the life of
my enemy Mussolini was in even greater danger than
he supposed. I came sooner than I had intended
because I became anxious about my sister." A very
black cloud passed over his face at those last words.
"She has just been here." He shuffled his feet,
crossed his legs and emitted a vast sigh. Rodney
was alert now, the soothing process had passed and
he was his own master just as the other failed a
little of self-control.

"But I must explain why I want you to join in
our councils. I have wished to get into touch with
your people either at Berne or at the Secretariat of
the League of Nations. But they won't so much as
listen to me for five minutes! They are pro-

Mussolini or they are afraid of being supposed to be anti-Mussolini, *or* they have no time to waste on back numbers like myself! Also I am a priest and not even the head of my party! Well, now, I wonder if you could help us—don't answer at once." Then, turning to Evriat, " Monsieur, my sister came to say one thing, only one. She looks very ill, she will not say where she has come from or where she is going to or who she has seen or will see. But she came to say that Mussolini must not come to Lausanne. If he will come to Switzerland for the conference in November it will be dangerous enough, but Lausanne is impossible."

He looked now from one to the other and Rodney watched Evriat whose thin lips were pressed together.

" But how does the Signora know ? "

" She does know," said Clemente simply. " But what's the use of a warning in such cases! Julius Cæsar was warned enough if Shakespeare can be trusted! No, the English must arrange that their Foreign Minister should object to Lausanne—at the last moment all the better. Mussolini would not refuse Genoa or Montreux—why not Montreux ? "

" But really," said Evriat with icy politeness, " you must not take this information for gospel truth. I for one am sure that Montreux for instance is a greater danger. The Signora may have received the information from people who have the best reasons in the world for deceiving her. The police in Lausanne are excellent, probably their precautions are already taken."

FIRST AID FOR THE DEAD

" I on the other hand am convinced that the information is true," said Rodney hotly, " only how on earth can I get anybody to listen to an obscure Oxford don ! If I knew the Foreign Minister or Sir Eric Drummond, but I don't. Still there might be a way. I might try the Foreign Office in London. I do know one or two men there. I wish I could see the Signora and get a little more information. May I say that you and M. Evriat would be willing to impart information ? "

" But I have no information about Lausanne and so how can I impart it ? " said Evriat sharply.

The telephone was the next sound and the Frenchman took up the receiver.

" It is for you—the Signora."

Rodney put his elbows on the table and leant his head on his hands. He could hear, he fancied, an echo of the voice. Then from Clemente himself such rapid Italian, soft and low, that it was surprising that he could understand even a few words— some expression of horror and grief.

Clemente put up the receiver. "The wicked woman is dead." For Evriat clearly that was enough. " She died on the train between this and Lucerne."

Then to Rodney's surprise, the big priest turned to where an ivory crucifix hung on the wall, knelt down in front of it and repeated the *Miserere* and the *De Profundis*. Evriat had knelt also and Castle had remained with his head buried in his hands. The rapidity of this first aid to the departed soul, Clemente's voice, the wonder of the words in their mystical humiliation allied to triumph, suited Rodney's needs at the moment.

The other two looked brisk and practical as they sat down.

" But who was she ? "

" A Red of the Reds who was in the Revolutionary government, exiled from Russia," said Evriat.

" A deformed cripple and a born orator," said Clemente.

" A terrific snob, hating the great and adoring their grandeur. I hear she never looked so hideous as when she lolled on the ex-Czarina's cushions in her motor."

" A former friend of Mussolini, who hated him more than any of the enemies who had never been his friends."

" I knew she was in Lucerne wearing gorgeous clothes worn shabby, and jewels that she was selling one by one."

Rodney had carried Patsey's sketch book. " Is that she ? " he enquired, holding it out to the others.

" Yes, the remains of her," said the Frenchman. " And I, who speak to you, I have been thrilled by the little monster."

" She died on the train—was anyone with her ? "

" A young English lady coming from Basel was the only person in the compartment."

CHAPTER VIII

PATSEY'S EVIDENCE

LADY LAVINGTON had gone to bed and to sleep after Sir John had insisted that he would meet Patsey at the station and bring her safely. When she was called next morning, the maid asked her to see Sir John as soon as she could be ready. It was for her very unusually early when she hurried downstairs and found the General in the dining-room.

"Patsey is all right," he began, "and is now having a bath, but we have neither of us been to bed. We were kept three hours at the station by those confounded Swiss police. And all the time Patsey was shut up in the big waiting-room with them, and I could only get some kind of information from the Consul occasionally."

He then himself gave some kind of explanation to the horrified Lady Lavington of what had happened. A Bolshevik dying alone with Patsey, and the poor child the only witness of the actual death at the inquest.

"I must go up and see how she is," she cried, as he seemed to have finished.

"I wouldn't," said the other kindly. "I don't think she wants sympathy. She is on the other tack, as girls often are nowadays. Follow her lead. Ah, here she is ! "

At that moment Patsey appeared, dressed in her prettiest morning frock and a blue hat. Nothing could have looked more light and airy, at a little distance at any rate. She held her head high, and only bent it for a moment to receive a kiss from her aunt.

Lady Lavington did not speak at all as she watched her anxiously. Patsey drank her coffee greedily and then began to talk in a rather shrill voice.

" They were so fearfully military, Sir John. Knowing you had not prepared me for such soldierly people."

Sir John laughed for the first time that morning.

" The men who never go to war are always like that."

" Well, it felt like a court-martial. I am sure I expected to hear ' Off with her head ' at any moment."

" What did they want to know ? "

" Well, Aunt Mary, they wanted to know why I had chosen the poor little monster to travel with and all my previous relations with her. However the Consul repeated my remarks in forcible German. Then they turned their attention to my private character, and wished to know why it was my custom to travel alone at night."

" It was disgraceful of Castle ! "

" Well, Sir John, accidents do happen, and the train did start on the stroke."

PATSEY'S EVIDENCE

" Did you tell them Castle had just missed the train ? "

" No, for this reason. It seemed to me that if those fidgetty Fascists made a fuss about Rodney and the lady to whom he gave a lift to Chiasso, and told lies about her having no passport, I had better not bring him in. They might think we were all tarred with the Red brush." At this both the elders were struck with admiration. " They did ask me why I had gone to Basel and I said I wanted to see the Cathedral. I then told them that no English girl would be afraid to go that short journey alone, but that I did think it extraordinary that no one came when I rang the bell. Seeing they did not like that, I went on to say that the poor little monster might have been saved if I could have got help. The Consul played up to that, and said he considered that this English lady had been put in a very dangerous position, and so they had a few minutes' quarrel with him—not, you know, exciting like Italians quarrelling—they are a stodgy lot here."

" How much of it will be in the papers ? " sighed Aunt Mary.

" There were no newspaper people allowed in, so the Consul said."

" He tells me this morning," said Sir John, " that the police want information about the Bolshies here, and what they can find out will be kept secret. The papers will have plenty of dramatic stuff about her past life in their pigeon-holes to fill columns. She seems to have been an astonishing character."

Lady Mary noticed that Patsey winced and lost colour.

" You must rest, child."

Patsey got up. " I've rested and it's no use. If you don't mind I think I'll go out. Don't come, Aunt Mary, honestly I think I'd rather go alone."

She bent over Lady Mary for a moment and her young sunburnt hand slipped into the wrinkled, worn old fingers. She knew Aunt Mary would understand in her own way.

Patsey with her long nervous stride covered the short distance to the Hofkirche in a few minutes. What a world apart it was from the ethos of the hotels, the literal obvious acceptance of the Christian tradition that the interior expressed. No mystical half lights, no half-concealed altars with dim lamps, no grouping of arches suggesting vistas beyond, all here was ordinary daylight shining on painted and gilded wooden figures, most quaintly domestic.

To Patsey there was something half consciously reassuring in the commonsense idealism of it all— here the facts of life had been so persistently faced and accepted. Rodney, who had come in by the north door, was standing with a handbook held upside down, apparently studying the curious carving of the stable at Bethlehem. Patsey sat on a bench at the bottom of the Cathedral until she felt sure it was safe to join him. Four poor women were the only others present and they were stolidly or solidly praying.

The conscience-stricken Rodney realised at once

that things were worse with Patsey than he had feared. She had betrayed nothing on the telephone two hours ago. As soon as he had reached his own hotel in the early morning, he had found a message asking him to ring Patsey as soon as he arrived. Then he had taken the orders he was now obeying.

" I told you to come here," said Patsey, " because you must not come to us. I must explain it all."

She pressed her hand on her forehead.

" You must sit down first," he said.

" Yes, thank you." They sat on the nearest bench. Patsey spoke in a quick low voice.

" I have managed to keep Gemma out of it with the police; they were nice and stupid really. They asked me what the woman had said and if she had mentioned anybody, and the Consul told them that I could not understand Russian and that satisfied them. But if you come in you will be a link with Gemma. She was talking to her all the time. Only for a minute did she see that I was not Gemma. She was begging and threatening Gemma : ' Kill or be killed,' she said once. And then "—Patsey turned round and looked at him with great eyes in her deadly white little face—" her last words were ' Piccolo Benito Mussolini traditore, nessuna pietà.' She died saying ' No mercy.' "

Patsey's whisper was on a sharp note, and a moment after she was leaning her head on the bench in front of her, shaken by tearless sobs. " I had never seen anyone die, I had never seen anyone dead."

"Oh, Patsey, I can't forgive myself for your having suffered like this!"

And then Rodney talked on instinctively, trying with lame obvious things to soften the horror. Presently the tears came and still he talked, very conscious of the futilities he spoke as to life and hope. Then he told of Don Clemente and how the news of the death came, and of the priest saying the *Miserere* in front of the Crucifix. She suddenly looked up at that.

"He prayed for her—he thought it was of use? Go on talking, Rodney."

So he told her everything and how Gemma had been upstairs overhead while he was in the little house and how he had heard her voice, dim though the sound was, while Don Clemente held the telephone. Last of all he told her of Gemma's warning. Mussolini must not go to Lausanne. He had not much more to tell as he had left the two men disputing when he had heard that a young English lady had been in the same carriage. He had hurried to the station in sudden panic of again missing the train.

"So the little Frenchman warned you against Gemma too!"

"It makes not the slightest difference."

"Of course not."

"Gemma's warning must get through."

Patsey was resuming her ordinary manner. "I think you would do more good in London and I shall get Aunt Mary to take me to Geneva."

PATSEY'S EVIDENCE

Such large designs and decisions as they came to
were tonic to Patsey, and when they had to part she
said firmly—" I won't think and I mean to sleep.
One must keep well. Don't comment on my next
remark. Aunt Mary is sorry that I have lost my
sketch book, and I am so glad. You see the sketch
of Gemma is on the next page. Now you go out by
the north door after you have studied the wooden
figures thoroughly and turn to the east ; and I go out
by the west door, a woman with her face to the west.
Good-bye."

She walked down the Cathedral with long uneven
steps and her head as high as usual, while Rodney
watched and was even now deceived by appear-
ances.

The short walk from the Hofkirche to the
Schweizerhof was long enough for Patsey to become conscious that the talk with Rodney had not
been what she had hoped for when she had set out
an hour before. It was true they had had much
to say and had been fully in touch with each other
while saying it. But though he had been kind—
awfully kind—it did seem to Patsey that he had
really said very little as to his desertion of the
night before. Sir John had been furiously angry
and Patsey had been prepared to be generously
forgiving.

In reality Rodney had played but a poor part and
had now a very poor rôle assigned to him. Patsey
herself had merely asked him to take himself away
to England. He was the only person in whom she

could confide and as fellow conspirators there was no falling off in her confidence in him. But—with a capital *B*—the drama of the situation was getting painfully oppressive to Patsey—and Rodney was certainly out of it for the moment.

BOOK III

CHAPTER I

RECOURSE TO GENEVA

IT was not the business of the Secretariat of the League of Nations to secure the personal safety of Signor Mussolini if he came to Switzerland. Patsey was aware of this; but as she knew no one at Berne, and as her aunt was closely connected with a very important member of the Secretariat, she had decided to make her next move to Geneva. Lady Lavington agreed willingly as she wished to get away from Lucerne and did not want to go home. It was a great point that Patsey's international interests fell in with Lady Lavington's convenience. An elderly widow living alone turns her activities very much towards self-protection and spoils herself when there is no one else to spoil. So she left Lucerne and all the horrid things Patsey had been through there, not knowing that she was being moved across Switzerland with a view to her niece assisting to protect Signor Mussolini. But she did know of a perfect hotel with a view over the water and an admirable chef.

Patsey, nervous and important, urged Aunt Mary to get into touch with the Secretariat, but Aunt Mary was not really intimate with her important cousin and did not want to rush him. The girl cousins however descended on Patsey eagerly. She had always dominated her special circle of contemporaries and now she was a little bit of a heroine. Aunt Mary had said it was a mistake to make a mystery about what had happened on the train, which in other words meant that she would make an interesting story of what dear little Patsey had been through to her friends and relations.

Two very pretty, charmingly dressed young women who could tell you all about foreign affairs when they were not playing tennis were the first questioners.

" Did you really see the Bolshie woman die ? "

" Oh rather," said Patsey airily. " I'm inclined to think that I killed her. I gave her some drops out of a bottle and it may have been poison."

" But the doctors said that she died of heart failure," objected the eldest cousin.

" Of course ! Did you ever hear of a case in which the doctors did not say that ? " Patsey was scornful. " I have no remorse for my first murder," she went on. " I am not the least morbid about it. I had no idea that I was ridding the world of a monster, so I was an unconscious benefactor to the human race. Charlotte Corday was always a heroine of mine."

" Did she look very horrid, Patsey ? " the younger of the two sisters asked in a low, awestruck voice.

" Oh no. I mean I don't suppose she was more of a corpse than other people. I was looking more at her clothes and I was horridly tempted to take her pearls. In fact it was the pearls made me give her the drops! My subconscious self is very fond of pearls."

One after another the younger members of the circle, male and female, got more and more outrageous statements from Patsey and told them to each other. But it was not long before Patsey passed into a phase of unpopularity—a new thing in her life. She could not be relied on to turn up for tennis or dancing or anything else, she was nervy about her health and had headaches or thought she had; she went into the moon when you were telling her things; she seemed to think that no one was worth listening to except herself; she was "running after" a very popular rich man who had just come from Rome and she did it crudely.

Aunt Mary was enjoying herself thoroughly, the important cousin's wife was delightful and she had quite a number of elderly engagements while she knew the young people were enjoying themselves.

" But, Patsey, I thought you were out at a dance with the others? " Lady Lavington took off her silk wrap and stood by her niece who was lying on a sofa.

" I had a headache, Aunt Mary, and I simply can't stand jazz music—if you want me to have a nerve breakdown give me a week of this jazz stuff! "

" But it's *the* music people like to dance to! "

" Yes, I know, but what's happened to people I don't know. It's blatant, brutal, savage idiocy—just mimicking niggers! "

I   129

THE SHADOW OF MUSSOLINI

"I don't like it," said Lady Lavington. "I liked the old romantic moonlight sort of things."

Patsey laughed and then groaned: "I tried last night and the thing seemed to be beating on my brain, and my brain was a wretched cracked gong—and the man I danced with imitated a nigger in a cockney voice singing 'I'm sitting on top of the world.' It was the limit."

Aunt Mary was not troubled with too much imagination, but she began to wonder if Patsey were a bit overstrained.

"But I don't like you to spend the evening here all alone."

Patsey did not explain that she had not spent the evening alone. The young man she was accused of pursuing had been with her part of the time.

"It's awfully kind of you to let me come," Dick Milward had said, not without condescension. He was a fine creature to look at and no fool—and Patsey had been really very forthcoming, and more crude than the rules of the game as usually played allowed.

"On the contrary," said Patsey in the grand manner, or perhaps the grand voice, for the manner was that of a very thin modern girl sitting on a high chair showing her legs and lighting a cigarette. "On the contrary it is very good of you to spare the time, but it's not safe to speak about some things in most places—this room is now empty as well as large. I have been trying, as you must have observed, to see you alone because I believe you are devoted to Benito Mussolini. Don't look alarmed. I don't want you to get me his signature, it's only that I want to give you a warning."

" Against Mussolini," he laughed. " Oh I get plenty of that ! I suppose I could tell you everything, however absurd, there is to be said against him."

" No, it's not that I can assure you. It is a warning for his sake ; you needn't smile, of course you also know much more than I can as to the endless warnings he receives. But has he been told he must not come to Lausanne for the Conference ? "

" Of course he has," laughed the other. " What does he care ? Besides half these warnings come from the Bolshies themselves. They head him off one place where the police can really guard him to another where they will be unprepared. I don't mind your knowing that I am in touch with the Lausanne police myself and nothing could be sounder than their attitude."

" Well, I've warned you," Patsey grumbled.

" And now please tell me why ? " he answered The manner of his question was stern.

Patsey waved her hand, a very small thin hand, in his direction. " You say it's of no consequence and then you expect me to tell you what I certainly shall not tell you."

" Oh, well, it can't matter really ! "

" Oh no, of course not. Let us leave it all alone until after Signor Mussolini has left Lausanne ! "

" Has it anything to do with that death in the train ? Because if so I can assure you they have traced all that woman's associates—Russian, Swiss, Italian."

Patsey looked at him anxiously.

" Even you," he laughed lightly, " have come in for a detailed enquiry. I doubt if you could have gone straight home. They were quite pleased you came here."

" What can they want little me for ? "

" Just in case any suspicious characters try to see you. That is their mania. They think the Bolshies may want you to tell them more about her death. So I've just this one warning in grateful return for yours. Don't go about alone."

Patsey leant back with her eyes shut, racking her brain as to how to produce the faintest impression on this consequential personage who knew everything. She saw it was impossible and she had to submit with all the grace she could to some kindly advice. He liked her much better than he had before, her crude attentions to himself had been only a manifestation of the endless feminine wish to have a finger in the pie of the greater affairs of life. The only pinprick she made on his memory was her good-night :

" Good-night—I will tell you more when it is too late. I mean after the Conference at Lausanne."

CHAPTER II

DEPRESSION

PATSEY had now an incentive for taking lonely walks, namely that she had been warned against doing so. Then nobody else wished to do just what she wished at the moment that she wished it. So she visited the Cathedral and the Greek church and went on the water and poked about the streets. She had not been prepared for the stark Protestantism of the great bare Cathedral. There indeed, if anywhere, can be realised by what a violent external change the Reformation affected the imagination. From an architectural point of view the negative advantage in the interior is immense. Patsey went in by the south transept and remained happily ignorant of the classic horrors of the imposed façade. Inside no pious hand in the later centuries had meddled with the austere simplicity. It was a church ungarnished, it had not even an altar, unfurnished but for bare benches and the greatness of it was unimpaired. Patsey enjoyed herself :

" Here," she thought, " I can just learn what Gothic means." After twenty minutes or so of pure delight she became suddenly tired, as imaginative sightseers do, and she sat on a bench to rest. Then, suddenly weary and discouraged, she felt thrown

133

back on herself, an unhappy self. She looked up
again at the stern beauty of the arches and pillars
and along the line that drew the eye towards the
empty choir. There is nothing so easy to lose, so
hard to regain, as the transient unity between our
feelings and external beauty. She could not get
back to the distraction it had given her.

" It's so bare and empty," grumbled Patsey, " and
cold. Who could get out of themselves here ? I
don't believe those old Calvin people were really sick
of themselves." She leant her head against a pillar
behind her. " What am I to do ? I can't go on like
this—it's all jazz when I'm with people but I'm not
much better when I'm alone. They all think me such
a stuck-up selfish pig—not that that much matters.
I wonder what one will find out to have mattered—
what the little monster found out while she was still
holding my hand. I wish I could have just one long
talk with Gemma. I want someone very, very good
indeed. Well I can't stand this place any longer.
I think I'll move on."

So she came out and looked in at the shop windows
and bought an embroidered handkerchief and some
scent which she threw away as she crossed the
bridge. She counted twenty confectioners' shops
before she turned in at a little café and asked for a
cup of coffee. The confectioners' shops had such
awfully rich cakes ; the people of Geneva seemed to
wallow in all that is most aggresively luscious, she
could not face going in, she would rather have the
plain little shop. In the plain little shop she seemed

to be a surprise, and while she drank her coffee she saw that she was being watched with interest. She supposed that it was unusual for a girl of her age not to prefer eating sweet things at the pastrycook's. But presently the woman who had given her the coffee disappeared and produced a dirty little man, who had a long look at Patsey, but with that scrutiny he seemed to be contented.

That was not Patsey's only lonely walk, but it was not easy to find solitary places on either side of the water. But there were little boats to go out in with a nice silent old Swiss whose company was restful.

In those hours on the water Patsey need not conceal her troubles and could talk to herself as she could talk to no one else. Last winter she had been a fool, and on believing that her heart was badly wanted by Rodney Castle she had, without any fear, given it to him. There had been so much obvious unspoken admiration in his eyes, his voice and his manner. But it was not simply because he wanted her that he had drawn her to him. For Patsey had found it evident that this man was a very good man, and that was to her unconsciously as much a necessity if she were to marry as many men feel it to be a necessity in thinking of a woman. She had felt so at peace in his company, and then she had had a great idea of the learning he possessed—which she did not. She had liked his face, his voice, his way of talking better than anybody else's. It sounds so dull all that, so dry, but put a match to it and there may be plenty of heat.

135

And the heat once kindled was not easily damped by disappointment.

One evening late, out on the water, she wondered, not for the first time, whether she could not get the better of it. She had no sense of the duty of fidelity to an unrequited love, for that article of the lover's creed has been wisely dropped by the young for many years. But sometimes the thing itself won't drop.

Could she drop it ? She really didn't know.

" I believe I like him quite as much as when I thought he was in love with me, that's the tiresome part of it. Dear old innocent, I'm not sure he even knows he is in love with Gemma ! And good Heavens ! it's such a sudden notional affair ! It might go off again. But if it goes off, a lot of romance will go with it. Don't know what he'd have left for anybody else, that's the pity of it. It's a sad sort of world at best."

It might be a sad world but that evening it was very beautiful. The old Swiss had stopped to rest and the drops of water dripping from his oars were wonderfully bright in their shining as they fell into the shadow of the boat. It is doubtful if Patsey was any happier than a love-lorn maiden who had watched the same moon laying its witchery on the waves of the lake a hundred years ago. Both she and Patsey probably rather liked to lay the blame for the grey days of life on their higher feelings. In both, the fact that they tried to analyse those same feelings might be a symptom of recovery. But the girl

of a century ago was in closer touch with
nature perhaps and had a more distinct ideal.
Patsey had got her human nature, but she lacked
any definite ideal of what it was most beautiful to
be, and so the general scheme of things and her own
part of it was full of jolts and jars—the music of her
life was syncopated.

Then there was another experience besides love
for which she had no measure, the experience of
death. She had known many of her own generation
who died and died nobly. But the first death she
had actually seen had had no ennobling side to it.
There was nothing she could do to place it in any
scheme of the universe—nothing to explain it away.
The only thing she caught at was the report of Don
Clemente's *Miserere*. But even that? Did that
mean that this half human thing had been responsible, that Divine Justice awaited this misshapen bit of misery with more misery—and had
to be propitiated? What was wickedness? She
had felt wickedness, felt it in that woman as something horribly repellant to herself, something infinitely repellant to her spiritual life. Since then
when she thought of that woman she found herself
thinking : " Oh I must be good ! "

This evening she was feeling as if she must get
help—she could not believe there was no help. No
help in a world so glorious—so full of majestic order !
The rhythm of law, the poetry of obedience in the
earth and water was all about her, in them was a
harmony that was not syncopated.

"I must get help," said poor Patsey. She looked at the old boatman. And she said what she had not known was at the back of all her thoughts.

"Monsieur," she spoke very courteously, "does everyone here believe in God?"

"Oh no. Oh no, not in these days."

"But do you?"

"But yes, naturally."

"Why naturally?"

"Because I have been so much on the water. In the streets things are confused. But now I know so much of what God does." His voice was very firm.

"And it makes you good?"

The old man laughed: "Ah, *pour ça*, it takes a good deal to make a man good, you must not expect too much, Mademoiselle. God is more merciful than men! More merciful than Mademoiselle would be, although she is very kind."

"More merciful than men, more merciful than I am. Thank you," said Patsey. "I'll just freeze on to that," she added to herself. It was a cold modernism that ' freeze,' but it was expressive. Then she looked at the boatman.

"I'd love to give him such a *pourboire* that he could really enjoy himself! Bless him——"

Heaps of people might have said just the same to Patsey and been of no use to her. "God is more merciful than I am, that's the point. Oh what a beautiful, beautiful night!"

CHAPTER III

ARTHUR TEMPLE'S LAST PARTY

IF the Athenians always wanted something new, it is equally true that the English are always seeking someone new to admire. Arthur Temple had been right in supposing that his Mussolini repertoire illustrated would be an asset. He had come to London a little shaky and distinctly sad. The depression was partly caused by a doubt whether he ought to have stayed in Lucerne to help the Lavingtons, instead of coming away a week sooner than he had intended. He had had a dim unreasonable suspicion that there was a chain of some sort between himself as Rodney Castle's host and the dreadful little Bolshy who had died holding poor little Patsey's arm. Sir John had annoyed him by smiling a slight sardonic smile when he had told him he must leave at once for England as the Italian ambassador was expecting to see him in London. But his spirits soon rose. The ambassador proved to be quite friendly and had accepted an invitation to see his Mussolini collection one afternoon, even choosing a most convenient afternoon from Temple's point of view. It was a fortnight off and that gave time to prepare for a party to meet him, which would be at the date he had always

139

chosen for an afternoon party, just towards the close of the season. The year before, Temple's party had been one of his few failures—he had a doubly sad recognition of facts, first how many that used to come were dead, and secondly that in the new world after the war there seemed very little need for him. For many, many years he had achieved such a combination of celebrities from all worlds in the world of London. Their signed faded photographs still stood or hung in the one very large reception room which, with a very small bedroom, made up his London quarters. Even in the middle distance of his backward glance over the years those signed photos and the scores of famous composers and the water colours of known artists had been appreciated. But in the new world, in the blare of jazz music and in the glare of the new colouring, those scores and those faintly tinted studies would be thrown on the scrap heap. This year, strong in the prospect of Mussolini treasures and the Italian ambassador, Arthur Temple looked round the room and had not the courage to leave it all alone. He blushed more than once as he put away in a cupboard the things that had once been so hotly admired. He seemed to hear such charming women's voices saying that that little study of the sea by moonlight was "too, too delicious," or praising a delicate pencil study by a great lady of the then Prime Minister.

But all that was dead. " He felt chilly and grown old " when he let himself dream. He himself must go with the times—so he bought things in strong colours and put away the William Morris curtains and covers, and he bought some photos of the portraits of Augustus John. He overtired himself at this work. Also he went out too much, and he spent two tiring week-ends in country houses where he behaved as if he were well and strong.

Yes, enthusiasm for Mussolini was all the wear at the end of that London season. The ideal of exhausted imaginations was the strong man, while he was also the refuge from fear, the hope not only for wealth and stability but also for a healthy life and for the cure for unemployment. But clearly there had been no strong man of action vouchsafed to the British nation at that date, and lacking him at home, they hailed him even from afar. It was soothing for jarred and overstrung nerves and a delight for the sentimental hero-worshipper. To have a hero made it easier to believe in humanity.

Arthur Temple's engagement board, a large one, was nearly as full as in pre-war days when he had sent out invitations to meet Sarah Bernhardt. People praised him again who had forgotten him last year, said what was quite true, that he had a big heart in his little body. They also said that his vitality was wonderful, his health extraordinary—a sort of praise which implies that longevity is for some obscure reason a matter for moral admiration. In the midst of these crowded hours of excited life, Temple received a letter from Rodney Castle which made him frown with perplexity.

After very proper expressions as to how ashamed

he felt to trouble him, Rodney proceeded to approach him with no little skill, as the leading pro-Fascist, pro-Mussolini Englishman in London. There was a danger threatening the great man, and there was an appeal to Temple to help to avert it. The old man's annoyance with Castle had melted in the warmth and occupation he had found in London. But he wished to go cautiously. Would it be wise or safe to have a finger in this pie ? But on the other hand would it be wise or safe to ignore Castle's warning ? Probably at any other date in his life he would have seen that it was a mistake, but in his present excitement he simply sent a note to Castle asking him to the party to meet the Italian ambassador. It really was a bad failure of judgment, for though the ambassador had laughed at the idea that Temple could be suspect to the Fascists, it was tactless, to say the least, to have Rodney to meet him.

Rodney was astounded but glad, for here was the best bit of luck he had had yet, as he wrote to Patsey. He had had nothing satisfactory to report. The Foreign Office as represented by his friend was quite uninterested in warnings, or in this one in particular, and the extreme preparedness of Lausanne for the safety of *all* foreign statesmen was above suspicion. Rodney approached Temple's door with great eagerness and anxiety. The flat was on the ground floor and had its own imposing front door. Two or three motors were outside—nothing like a string, and yet he had surely not come too soon—it was nearly five o'clock. It was odd, but two servants were leaving cards, and the occupants of two motors drove away without getting out.

He reached the door while it was still opened and he was just going in, when the servant he had known at the Villa said, " There is no party to-day, sir. Mr. Temple is ill. Yes, sir, it is double pneumonia, sir. Would you come in ? The nurse would like to see you."

A man nurse who seemed to be in command explained that Mr. Temple wanted somebody and that he had spoken of Mr. Rodney Castle. Would he come in and see if he knew him ? Rodney followed into the big reception room and saw that the sick man's bed lay at one end, and at the other the tables on which the cups and saucers, the silver and the jugs and basins, were already laid out for the party. He was told afterwards that the old man had insisted on seeing everything made ready.

He had known the room and its old-world restful charm and was startled by the change. Orange and scarlet and silver now shone in the newness of the materials on all sides. The narrow bed and its faded coverlet looked strangely forlorn and out of place, and it reminded Rodney that Arthur Temple had not been personally luxurious.

" We brought him out of the little bedroom to give him more air. At first he could not make out where he was," said the man nurse, and the woman nurse added : " He repeated just now before he fell asleep as if he were angry : ' It's not my room, not my things ! ' but he has looked happier since the morning. He has not worried any more about the party. He still thinks they will all come. He said it would go off all right even if he could not get up." They had not watched the exhausted frame in its last living sleep for many minutes before he opened his eyes and noticed Castle—or so it seemed.

" I must apologise," he said, " for receiving you all in bed like this—please look after each other. The doctors insisted." Speech failed. Arthur Temple made one more great effort to do his duty by the party he clearly supposed to be in the room : " I would have put you off only the Duce is coming himself. I knew the Princess and all of you would like to meet him. Here he is just coming. Nurse, I must get up. I can't receive——" He tried to sit up, gasping for air, and then he cried : " Mussolini " before he died without any further struggle.

The old Italian valet, about whom so many charming stories had been told for fifty years past, wept his old man's little tears and was easily persuaded to go to bed. Rodney did not like to fly at once, he sat down at a little distance because the nurse asked him to wait for the doctor. During the quarter of an hour he stayed, the bell kept on ringing and the telephone sounding in the hall. Rodney wondered how many of this crowd as they drove away or received news of the end at home would feel any sorrow or pity for the little man who had made one more effort to keep his place among them. He did not know how great an effort it had been to find a foothold on the slippery social descent. For that foothold he had put away the records of a happier past and dishonoured its relics, and for that foothold he had exploited his real hero-worship—the strongest sentiment of his old age. There on the table most neatly arranged was the portfolio and all the portraits of Mussolini and a model of a bust of the Duce, and neat little sketches of his own of Fascisti. Rodney felt that Arthur Temple had tried in vain to get a big thing, which he had had the sense to recognise, measured by his own compasses. And there was the irony of it, that this little man had been formed once and for all by the Liberal school of the nineteenth century and had fallen down before the one man who had had the courage to overthrow its doctrines.

"Strange," he wrote to Patsey afterwards, " how the extremes meet, the wicked Bolshevist woman and the good little drawing-room gentleman both died obsessed by the thought of Mussolini.

> ' Why man he doth bestride the narrow world
> Like a colossus . . .' "

CHAPTER IV

After the Party

RODNEY attended the putting away of the small remains of Arthur Temple in the large black marble tomb erected by his father, who had made the money the son had so greatly enjoyed.

There were two or three men present and a little dowdy old lady who was the chief mourner. He identified nobody and was walking away through the vast crowd of graves when he was accosted by a total stranger, who greeted him in very poor English.

" Excuse me but how do you know me ? "

" I heard you give your name just now and I wished with you to speak."

Having agreed to communicate in French, Rodney asked him his business.

The man was young, thin and fair, with large bright eyes and a very pleasant mouth. He was it seemed a musician who should have played at the party which was stopped by Temple being called away " to where," said the stranger, " he will hear better music I understand even than mine." He went on to remark that he had only come to London recently, and only recently been obliged to use his music to support himself :

AFTER THE PARTY

" I was coming to Oxford to call on you. That will not be necessary if you can give me an hour now. You saw Don Clemente in Basel." After that a taxi took them to Rodney's club and as they went the young man began by talking about himself as young men will. He belonged to the Partito Popolare, he wished the genius at its head were not a priest. It was a drawback—they would have done much more under a lay leader, the younger men did not care for a party in the sacristy, but there had been no lay-man of sufficient distinction, " and after all our head is a real genius, the power of seeing a situation is supremely his, no one can doubt that who witnessed the greatness and rapidity of our success. Don Clemente is a voice and a holy man but of organisation he knows nothing, he has beautiful dreams but he does not tire himself to go into details that one ! "

The young man then returned to his own views : he was an ardent Catholic, he was a lover of liberty, his countrymen were falling down before a tyrant who persuaded them he was a liberator, and so on and so on. But Rodney, impatient as he was to know why the man had wanted to see him, was rather attracted than repelled.

The youth was ardent, keen and with a sense of humour ; also he was like an Englishman in the combination of reverence towards his leaders mingled with criticism. For the rest he insisted that the party to which he belonged were not now in action :

" We will give the Duce five or even six years, and by then when the country is normal they must allow constitutional action and we ask for nothing more. But we do resist the general muzzling order! We are not plotters, but Heaven help us, Italians would never have conceived or endured the Spanish Inquisition; they won't endure a Mussolini Grand Inquisitor either."

Arrived at the club and with ice tinkling in his white wine, the stranger drank and was silent for a few moments.

"I wrote to your leader a private letter," said Rodney, "and I have had no answer."

"I am the answer," replied the other. "I hope you will excuse this when you understand. You wrote as a friend of a lady who is no longer a friend of ours."

"Impossible!" exclaimed Rodney.

"She has cut herself off and we must cut her off. Clemente will not believe it. But she persists in going about Switzerland with the most appalling scoundrels. He saw her once, but she refuses to see him again; he implored her to come right away, but she would not. She has chosen her own path—there is not the least doubt she has joined the Bolsheviks. Now for the credit of the Partito Popolare we can hold no communication with her. What she may do will be blamed on us. Clemente also, if he will not give her up, we must give up."

"But she has given her life to your ideals; she hates the Bolsheviks."

"That may have been true once, but now! See, she could have got away easily! No one knows

better than she does how we have fought and will
fight Bolshevism. A tragedy, yes. But we can't
waste time on tragedies, there are too many."

" I wrote to say—— " interrupted Castle.

" No need to tell me. I would rather not know,
the only answer is that there is no communication."
He cut the air with his hand, a sharp decisive gesture
and Castle felt the hardness of the Latin nature in
his cheerful smile. So the Fascisti cut Gemma off
on one side and the Popolari on the other !

" She was a great woman and a beautiful soul,"
concluded the Italian lightly. " She was an inspiration to me and to many of us. But nobody lives
long in these days without seeing an angel or two
fall from heaven."

Rodney saw him go with a sense of relief—and the
next moment he became indignant. How could they
desert Gemma like this, for that was what they
were doing ! They might say they had given her
an opening to come back, but how did they know
what hold these brutes had got of her. Clearly she
had no friends but Don Clemente, who would soon
be far away, Patsey and himself. " An inspiration "
—the ungrateful brutes—he could well understand that she had been an inspiration ; it was as
an inspiration he would always think of her, the
companion of that wonderful journey. He sat on
that breathless July day in his club a very sad man.
All the world was dull, wretched, unprofitable.

CHAPTER V

THE TWO SCRAPBASKETS

RODNEY sat down with a grim smile to face the mass of papers on his writing table. Here in Oxford he had intended to have a quiet time to work at the two editions of the classics he was preparing for the Clarendon Press, he had come back for that purpose. But before everything else a man is bound to open his post, and Rodney's had accumulated ever since he had left Italy.

Weary, weary work it was, not so much to divide the grain from the chaff as to put on one side the lowest minimum that he must attend to of either. A huge basket was soon filled with advertisements that obviously could be disregarded, but they had a growing effect on his mind as he threw them away. The depressing thought of the labour that had gone to fill up thousands of baskets such as this all through the country—the enormous number of men and women in their youth and vigour employed in this vast battle of persuasives, producing nothing but this huge volume of bought praise. What was the proportion of cost between the thing produced—the labour of making it—and the labour of advertisement ? That was sad enough in a world where labour was costly, but the disastrous effect on the minds of the men and women entirely occupied in such strange forms of persuasion ? He had another basket for appeals for causes which also made him sad, even sadder. Heavens, that second basket if taken seriously must have sent a man mad ! To be ignorant of human suffering is hardening, but to have all forms of it, and of animal suffering also, perpetually before the mind has either a hardening effect or produces a surface sensitive to everything while there is all the hardness of self-defence beneath. Added to which is the cynicism that is produced by any sense of over advertisement.

The basket of appeals was soon as full as the other. One thing was clear, whatever he, Rodney, could give away to relieve suffering would not be sent in answer to these appeals. He was generous, he was already helping where he could, and the awful contents of that basket and all they had cost had no effect whatever.

Meanwhile on the table was a growing heap of notes and notices and circulars as to concerns which he had more or less undertaken.

And now after the physical change and the enormous mental preoccupations of the past weeks, he felt the heap of things on the table to be proof of absolute folly. Had he really promised to take the chair for a lecture on psycho-analysis during the summer school ? Had he agreed to speak at the C.O.P.E.C. Conference at Birmingham on the prospects of Institutional Religion ? Surely he had not agreed to take part in a subsectional discussion at the same conference on Birth Control ? He must have been mad last winter, for he had also promised, it seemed, to speak on Disarmament to the League of Nations Union somewhere in the north. Then there were inter-University meetings, one involving two days at Sheffield in the early autumn. There were a whole number of impatient notes as to his part in the summer hospitalities at Oxford—he had said, it seemed, that he would help to entertain Checko-Slovaks and Danes and a Labour party from the Clyde—and incidentally and for once in a way some learned men were coming from Paris. Lastly there was an Italian party conducted by the Anglo-Italian League. Reaching that struck the first spark of interest. Were they Fascists, these professors from Pisa and Venice ? What were the intellectuals in Italy ? What did they think of the dictator ?

He sat with that notice in his hand for a longish time. As men do in times of disintegration and discouragement, his imagination escaped from his surroundings to the less known country with positive relief.

" Quack, quack, quack," seemed to come out of the wastepaper baskets in more or less silly voices, and more solemn " Quack, quack," came out of the letters and circulars on the table. He badly wanted an inspiration in his own life ; Oxford badly wanted one big genuine inspiration instead of a hundred thousand views ; England wanted a great spiritual inspiration instead of a hundred thousand plans for improvement. Then he sickened at the prospect of the autumn, especially at all the endless informal meetings he would be expected to attend. He felt so sick of Oxford, so sick of that pleasant work of teaching the classics, of preparing new editions of old books for the Clarendon Press, of discussions on the miraculous element in the Scriptures, of talks on psycho-analysis, of the proofs of faith-healing, of the phenomena of mysticism. " Quack, quack, quack," it all sounded in his ears to-night. What was wrong with Oxford especially ? He thought with a bitter smile of Newman's *Idea of a University*. Do you form men's minds by chatter, chatter ? Then the sentimentality ! There was a plan for getting funds for educating young Germans at Oxford at our own expense—and people were actually subscribing. And yet how many sons and daughters of men who died for England would never have such advantages ? It was only one instance out of hundreds of senti-mentality instead of justice. Surely if there were some big idea, some ideal involving self-denial, action, self-devotion, there would be less of this tosh. Italy had found its inspiration, but plainly the materials had been inflammable when Mussolini lit the spark, or had Don Sturzo set it smouldering and Mussolini stirred it into a big flame ? Anyhow it was alive. And yet England had sacrificed more, and suffered more, than Italy in the war. Had England had her baptism of blood without a new life ?

CHAPTER VI

THE ORDER OF THE DAY

" DEAR RODNEY,—

" Here we are back in Geneva. We finished
our four weeks at Aix and the waters have not done
Aunt Mary as much harm as she expected. It was
not easy to persuade her to come back. She enjoyed
herself so much here in July, but she said everybody
would be too busy with the meetings of the League
of Nations to think of us. But I told her that as all
the lunatics from all the world come here on these
occasions we might find somebody amusing. So far
I must own it has proved ghastly dull. Aunt Mary
for a wonder was not well so I went alone to the first
Séance. I had a ticket for the gallery in the Salle
de la Reformation, which looks like a dissenting
chapel. You never saw such queer people as there
were in the galleries. I had heard that every crank
in the round world gets here sooner or later, with the
hope of imposing some pet scheme on the Universe.
Certainly with a few exceptions they looked as if
they were suffering from *idées fixes* or megalomania.
By the way I suppose I was there because I am
really suffering from both.

" When the speeches began I had the feeling that
the speakers had to go on explaining their intense

belief in the League of Nations because they were so very doubtful about it. A queer, queer thing all the elaborate ugliness of the mechanism of it, for it's really fearfully sentimental, don't you think ? If they only remembered that ritual and beauty do matter. It was all as ugly as a counting-house and appallingly monotonous. A long speech almost interesting in French seemed double the length and awfully dull badly translated into English. And the one speech that showed a real apostle—a real crusader, anything else you like to call him—was put from fine English into bad French by a Swiss with the expression of a cow and the voice of a gramophone.

" The choice of the President and the representatives of all the countries for the year took ever so long. Then two men read notices, each one ending in the words ' l'ordre du jour,' like a loud Amen.

" I went to sleep wondering if ' l'ordre du jour ' was a hammer beating on the top of my head. I woke feeling as if I were being watched, and I saw the nasty little man I told you about who had watched me like a cat when I was in his café. I shan't get to see anybody of any use I'm afraid, everybody seems to be rushing after ' l'ordre du jour ' as if it were the snark. I just saw Dick Milward and he asked if he could come to the hotel some evening. He had been among the important people on the benches on the floor of the hall. I don't know why, but there are unimportant people who have that knack. He looked nice, I must say, but all our men looked more distinguished than all the others it seemed to unprejudiced me !

" Well, if I've no more news for you I suppose you have none for me ! "

This letter was more cheerful than any that Patsey had written from Aix. Like the man whose tombstone bore the words : " I was well but I wanted to be better and so I came here," Lady Lavington, not content with fair health, had wanted to be better. Unlike the man of the candid tombstone, she survived the treatment at Aix but she was a poorer thing in consequence.

To Patsey, August had been a long penance. Indeed the two of them had suffered and their morale was considerably lowered by heat and a total absence of excitement. In reality Patsey got some good out of those dreadful weeks, for dullness was what her nerves were in need of. So on coming back to Geneva she was more herself than when she had left it. At first, as she had said in her letter, it was dull enough, and the first evening when she was asked to dance at the house of a popular Englishman she was unfeignedly glad.

" It will probably be all jazz," said Lady Lavington.

" Oh, jazz has its charms after all," laughed Patsey.

And it was a jazz band tinkling and braying its noise far into the exquisite garden, insulting the moonlight that was lighting the glories of the mountain and the lake. Patsey was in the same irreverent mood, determined to have fun, knowing that she was in good looks, pleased and pleasing.

The evening was no longer young when Dick Milward came in and stood in the doorway.

" He always looks as if he could only be spared five minutes for recreation by the Council of the League," said her partner to Patsey, " and yet he has not even got a job here."

" Yes, but he does know about things."

" Or thinks he does. But he has got up this Mussolini stunt you know, and so when people want to know things that nobody knows about the great man they ask him."

Patsey laughed, for she was thinking of what she had done herself as to this young man and the great warning : " Why don't you like him ? "

" Well, I don't know, but he has really too much to him if you know what I mean. He is a sort of high-brow political author, then he is a great fine guardsman sort of fellow who is always rubbing it in that he does not give himself airs, and he is rich and not lazy, it's too much altogether. I like things divided up more, don't you ? "

" He also dances almost as well as you do," added Patsey.

And during the next dance, which was with the man of too many parts, she decided that he danced better than anyone she knew. They danced and danced to their mutual advantage, the most observed couple in the room. Patsey felt the crazy jazz more

THE SHADOW OF MUSSOLINI

and more an incentive and means to get away. Surely that insistent clash, crushing the mere suggestions of romance and feeling in the music, that " dance, dance I tell you for fear you should think," was an escape. When they went out to breathe in the moonlight Patsey's eyes shone.

" I was kept so late by——" he mentioned several very important people, with cheerful and obvious enjoyment. " But I was in hopes of seeing you here and asking you more about the great warning. I told them that duty called me away."

" Go on," said Patsey, " I don't mind. If you are sorry afterwards I won't even say ' I told you so.' "

" You are very magnanimous."

" It's my nature," said Patsey modestly.

" But seriously have you had any more news of the Lausanne conspiracy."

" Seriously if I have, I shall not tell you."

" Who would you tell ? "

" I might confide in Signor Mussolini, but after the way my effort was received by you, I am discouraged. And yet you know, if he knew that I murdered the poor little monster, he might be grateful."

" You murdered——"

" I gave her some drops and I believe those drops to have done the job."

" Really, Patsey, you are heartless."

" Really, Dick, though I didn't know we called names, I am so hot that unless we go on dancing I shall have time to faint."

THE ORDER OF THE DAY

" Yes, in one moment ; but what would you tell the Duce if you saw him ? "

" What I certainly shall not tell you—the last words of the little monster for one thing, but other things too."

She got up, swept round towards the open window where a callow youth was impatiently awaiting her, and the great Dick showed some simplicity or some swagger for he waited without disguise to get another dance with Patsey, but he waited in vain.

CHAPTER VII

In the Queer Little Café

If Patsey had read all the stories that have ever been written about Bolsheviks and decoys and thieves and murderers, she would have done the silly thing all the same. She had read enough in all conscience to know that it was an idiotic proceeding. The temptation had come in a dirty envelope on the tray of early morning *café au lait*, and it was expressed in a few words written in pencil in a backhand :

" If you take another cup of coffee at the same café at six o'clock you will meet Gemma."

Yet Patsey felt a little chilly about it, it was like a nasty draught in a pleasant warm room. The *joie de vivre*, that had suddenly revived the night of the first September dance in Geneva, had inclined her to forget Gemma and had helped her to drive out of her mind the horror of the awful experience of death. Perhaps she wanted a change of air even from the atmosphere of deep feeling altogether. It was more amusing to be admired by Dick Milward than to be very serious about anybody. It was Dick who most unconsciously helped her to get off by herself to the little café before six o'clock. He had 'come to tea with Lady Lavington who was very friendly indeed. A girl friend who showed no signs of leaving had absorbed Patsey for an interminable three-quarters of an hour. Then Patsey suddenly asked him if it were too late to go and see the Cathedral, was it true that it shut at five o'clock ? He wildly asserted that it shut at seven and offered to show her the way. Patsey instantly flung her girl friend into the arms of her aunt, and proceeded to lead Dick out of the hotel.

" I know that the Cathedral has been shut for twenty minutes," she said. " Dick I hope you won't mind, it was the only way to get out."

Dick's happy smile soon turned into undisguised temper as he found that he was being dismissed—that Patsey wanted to walk away alone.

" I told you you ought not to go about Geneva by yourself. I am coming with you."

" My dear Dick I am always going about alone, and, as those who have undertaken the charge of this orphan girl make no objection, I shall continue to do so."

" You are so childish, Patsey ! You have been in one bad scrape, why can't one get you to see sense. My goodness ! I wouldn't be the man to take care of you ! "

" Forbid it heaven ! " ejaculated Patsey and then he raged—for a few minutes full of ejaculations and expletives. His usually serene and slightly conse-quential expression was clouded to blackness as he strode along beside her.

" Here comes," said Patsey gently, " a very im-portant member of the permanent Council. I should be sorry for him to see you looking like that, it might give him a false impression that you are sometimes a little unbalanced." Then she stopped just before the great man reached them, held out her hand and with ringing clearness bade him good-bye. She strode away too rapidly to know what befell Dick—the point was that she had escaped.

The little café was empty as she reached it, only five minutes past six o'clock. Then the woman she had seen before came out and looked at her and, as on the former occasion, went away and brought in the dirty little man. They then asked her very politely in French to go into the back room, but this she declined to do. They consulted together and then brought out a large screen which they put round the corner near the door, enclosing a table and two chairs. They did not seem mysterious or excited only rather dull and heavy and unpleasant. It seemed absurd to refuse to go behind the screen, and directly she had sat down on one chair a woman who came in hastily from the back room sat on the other.

" You should not have come here," she spoke in a low tone in English. " I am going to ask you a few questions in French. If you can answer out loud all the better.

" You were in the train when a certain woman died. What did she say ? "

" She thought I was somebody called Gemma, she asked for medicine, ten drops, and I gave them to her. She spoke last of all to Mussolini, and to him she said, ' Piccolo Benito Mussolini, nessuna pietà.' "

IN THE QUEER LITTLE CAFÉ

Gemma's face seemed almost as stolid as the other faces in the café:

" You learnt nothing from her as to plans or arrangements ? "

" Nothing."

" What did she wear ? "

Patsey ticked the list off quickly: " The cloak was sable though it was a warm evening. When it fell back I saw magnificent pearls, two strings. The dress was of silk, old-fashioned. The dressing-case fittings had jewels set in them."

" Did you keep anything ? "

Patsey reddened and stared.

" Remember it would be dangerous," the dull voice went on, " not to speak the truth here."

" I had no chance," said Patsey in as matter of course a manner as possible. "She was only just dead and still clutching my wrist when the guard found us."

" Then the police have the jewels ? "

" Of course."

" Thank you, that is all, I think," and then she whispered in English: " Lean hard against the screen, push, then go at once. I shall be in the Cathedral to-morrow at three. Now be quick."

The screen fell with a bang and Patsey remained in full view from the street. A policeman passing outside heard the noise and saw the young lady come out. He found the master of the café scolding his wife for knocking over the screen, while she retorted that no one but an idiot could have put it just opposite the door.

CHAPTER VIII

The Great Warning

" Dear Rodney,—

"I have much to tell but nothing very cheerful ; indeed I feel more depressed than I can say ! I went to the Cathedral at three o'clock and to be reasonably careful, as I really intend to be, I took a taxi with a man the hotel people know well and I told him to wait. I went in by the north transept. I saw Gemma near the door sitting on the nearest bench, but for a moment she did not see me.

"I was excited and I suppose startled her. She looked up at me as if she had been asleep and resented being woke up ! Then she pulled herself together and began to apologise. When I saw her in the café the light was bad, I did not see her properly, I was nervous in the horrid place and I was only there three minutes. But now I am miserable about her. If I had not seen her at Lucerne I should not have believed what you said of her beauty. Her clothes are very shabby and dusty, but that would not matter if she did not hold herself differently. I can't understand how the woman I drew so badly at Lucerne could lose all that I tried so hard to put into that drawing. I think she is ill for one thing, but that would not make her look ashamed—there's

164

no other word for it ! She began by being elaborately polite, which just put me off at the start.

"It was all a dreadful disappointment and I felt hurt, which was really absurd for she had nothing to thank me for, except for my agreeing to come and meet her there. Of course she does not know how I have stuck up for her all the time. She seemed more natural, although nervous, when she warned me not to go to the café again, and she told me just as Dick did not to go about by myself. For a moment then our eyes met and I did feel a real thrill. I had found her again. But then she became even more difficult, more strange. She asked me a series of abrupt questions almost rudely. She wanted to know more about the death in the train and she gave sharp sighs but paid no real attention to me myself. Once when I was telling her what the monster had said she repeated :

"' Kill or be killed ! ' and added, ' as if it were only that ! '

"Presently she wanted to know if you or I had done anything through the English authorities to prevent the Conference being held at Lausanne. I don't even know how she connected you with the warning unless Don Clemente had told her, or how she knew that I knew you at all ! Our total failure to get any attention to our warnings astonished her.

"' It seems so strange,' she said, ' to insist on having the Conference at Lausanne. Why should they ? '

" ' Why, because all the preparations are made. It is better prepared already than any place can be by the beginning of November.'

" ' Heavens,' she said, ' how can you *prepare* a whole town against a chance pistol shot ? I tell you, Miss Lavington, if there is a policeman at every window and in every cellar Benito Mussolini will die there ! It is one of the places where the police have been really deceived. What a muddle, how many idiots. If one could only get at himself, he has a *flair* for facts, for seeing a situation. He would not be where he is if he were an idiot. Oh for ten minutes alone with him ! I could save his life, I who speak to you. Oh the fools, the fools ! If he is murdered now, we are all ruined.'

" Rodney, she was still strange and paying little attention to me but she looked more herself—or what we know she really is.

" ' I am his enemy, but God knows no friend of his is more anxious to keep him alive. We are not ready to do without him. It would be chaos.'

" She was still mysterious but more natural, and bigger—you know what I mean ? Perhaps it was suggestion, I don't know, but an idea came into my mind and without stopping to think it over I let it out :

" ' Why couldn't I see him and tell him that he must see you ? '

" ' See Mussolini ! But how ? '

" I gave myself airs and said : ' Oh, by influence. I have an idea I know someone who would help—

he is quite, quite safe—I can but try, no harm done if I fail after all.'

"After that she was no longer inattentive to me. But all the same there was something too horribly, horribly painful and so sad. It was as if she could not or would not be natural or human. I could not touch her at all, there were bars up all the time. But do you know I feel it in my bones. I am quite sure that she will see Mussolini before the Conference, whether through my help or not! And then it will depend on himself whether he is saved or not! Anyhow I'll do what I can though I can't tell even you how I mean to do it."

CHAPTER IX

PATSEY TAKES ADVANTAGE

THE difficulty of pursuing one virtue is the danger to others. Patsey had a love of generosity and she had chosen to be very generous to Rodney and for his sake to take up Gemma's cause and fight for it. But in fact other virtues were somewhat disregarded in her relations with Dick. All is fair perhaps if you are in love yourself, but all is not fair to the person who is in love with you. Probably Patsey was not slow to discover that Dick was losing his valuable head where she was concerned. Aunt Mary thought this a much better opportunity than the last, and though she appeared to be quite unobservant when with Patsey, she could not pretend to ignore the observations of others looking on at the most interesting of human games.

The evening after the great disappointment of the meeting with Gemma, Patsey was glad to go out to dine at the Villa, where the younger cousins were living with their important parents. It was not to be a party. At first Patsey had been blamed for her crude efforts to annex Dick Milward, but now that he followed her " like a lamb " he added to her glory. Besides she was quite jolly and amusing since they had all been away for August.

PATSEY TAKES ADVANTAGE

" No one here to-night, Patsey—only our three little selves. We will sit out in the garden."

But the three little selves did not get to ten o'clock in the garden without interruption. And one of the two disturbers of their quiet was Dick Milward. It seemed a matter of course that the two girls of the house should take the second visitor for a stroll while Dick sat down next to Patsey.

" You look depressed."

" So do you."

" But why should you be depressed ? "

" Really the wildest of optimists would allow that even I might at moments feel depressed ! "

" Do you know what people say about you ? "

" Of course not. I have no sufficiently candid friend for that, thank Heaven ! "

" They say," Dick went on stolidly, " that if anybody tries to get intimate with you he or she knocks his " (" or her," interpolated Patsey)—" his or her head against a stone wall," finished Dick.

Patsey gave a pleased laugh : " I think I'm rather proud of that. It means I can keep a secret."

" *The great warning,*" laughed Dick.

Patsey suddenly spoke in deadly earnest after that. She was feeling rather badly about Gemma.

" Yes, the great warning, and about that I can't stand any chaff, it's too serious. Heaven knows I'm not keeping that to myself because I'm secretive or proud of it—but because I have come to despair of anybody listening to the truth."

" I am sorry," said Dick, now also very serious,

169

"you don't know how little I want to risk annoying you."

He betrayed all the truth of what he said as he looked at her. And indeed the very slim white figure wrapped tightly in a white silk shawl, the comely little head half turned away but just showing a pale cheek in the September gloom, the whole effect of her presence was to him very moving.

"I've made jokes and said horrid things; I know you all think me heartless," said Patsey who was feeling lonely, "and I can't say now what it was to see that poor woman die, and be alone and wonder if I did wrong. I suppose hiding that sort of thing is what makes the stone wall round me, but I'm not so very happy inside it."

"Patsey, I never imagined for one moment that you were heartless——"

"Then," Patsey interrupted, "I got this warning handed on and nobody will listen and time is getting on, only a few weeks now and he will come to Lausanne."

"But what can I do? You won't or can't convince me by telling me more. Just tell me what you do think I can do, and I promise you, if I possibly can, I'll do it. I would do a great deal to make you look happier."

And Patsey did it, did the old, old thing with the man who was delivered into her hands: "It's so simple," she said. "It is just to get me five minutes alone with Mussolini."

Dick was suddenly sobered and silent.

PATSEY TAKES ADVANTAGE

"Yes," he said firmly, after one moment for thought. "I believe I can do that. I don't pretend it's easy, and there's a risk for you. He and the people round him will either think you are one of a thousand lion-hunters after the greatest lion now alive, or that you are among the thousand or so women who want to conquer him as a mere man."

"I'll face all that. He will soon understand when he sees me, and for the others I care just that!"— and she snapped her fingers.

Dick was silent again—he very particularly disliked the job because he cared too much for her dignity to face her becoming absurd, and he also knew that he risked his own entirely unofficial position with the Duce, who had only recently taken a fancy to him. Oh well, after all if she were pleased—but he did wish she knew more of life and had not taken this fancy into her head.

Meanwhile Patsey was shaking a little and controlling the wish to jump up, to laugh loud and long, or do any other silly thing. She knew, much better than he supposed, that she had given him a hard task and her conscience was not perfectly easy. Their silence had become uncomfortable before he said with an effort to do it quite handsomely :

"I am to go to Florence next week, my mother is coming by the St. Gotthard. You could join her at Basel and come with her. I will ask him as soon as I can. But you know I must give him some reason, something besides *the* warning. That would only make him refuse."

"Tell him," said Patsey, "how I was with that woman when she died and that is why I want to see him."

"Well, I'll try that," said Dick. "It might answer. He was interested about her I know. I'll do my best," and then suddenly becoming cheerful, "I'll show you Florence really and truly, and we'll have a splendid time—won't we Patsey?"

Patsey's laugh was shrill and a little too loud, but to Dick it was all right. He had found a way to please her after all.

"But what will your mother say?"

"Oh she will love to have you," said Dick.

Patsey at this moment was more than merely glad that the others came chattering out of the wood close behind her.

BOOK IV

CHAPTER I

BETTER TO BE AN ORPHAN

EVERYBODY helped Patsey to deceive herself in the matter of the journey to Florence. Dick's mother had just been offered the loan of a famous villa in Fiesole. Nothing was said publicly about the hope of seeing the Italian Prime Minister, but Patsey was informed in a private letter that her conference with him would take place in the capital of Tuscany during the first week of her visit to Fiesole. In their excessive tact none of her circle betrayed to Patsey that they were expecting her engagement to Dick Milward to be announced at any moment. She herself was living in such an atmosphere of great issues and heroic designs that she overlooked the danger of misleading poor Dick. The present rules of the game allowed great latitude, and it would be absurd to say that you must marry a man because you went to Italy with his mother! Still if you knew he was in love and you were quite quite sure you never could return that love, might it not be kinder to give up the pleasure? If Patsey ever faced up to that question at all the answer would clearly be that she was not going for pleasure, she was moving from Geneva to Florence solely on her mission to save the life of Mussolini. Certainly all the enemies and all the friends of the

175

Duce must agree that on the thread of that life the state of Europe largely depended.

Small wonder then if Patsey walked on, her head a little higher than usual, and ignored the minor personal considerations that no one ventured to speak about. Dick had left Geneva immediately after the night of his promise to Patsey without seeing her again. About a week later Patsey joined Mrs. Milward at Basel, and they reached Florence via Milan the evening of the following day. The heat on the train had been very great, but Mrs. Milward, by an incredible amount of perspiration, and Patsey, owing to her extreme slimness, did not feel it excessive.

Mrs. Milward was one of those women about whom almost anything could be said in a lady's newspaper. She was at different times a keen worker for all sorts of charities, for the Liberal Party, for musical competitions. She was indefatigable for at least three weeks in the year in helping every sort of institution in her own neighbourhood, which depended on her entirely for that space of time. She always had a family party at Christmas, after which she usually went to India or Cairo or America, and was also a popular hostess in the season when she was back in London. After all of which taken together it need hardly be said that she was exceedingly practical, and that her greatest gift was for getting work out of other people—but that her secretaries adored her was really not the case. She was enormously rich, amazingly strong in body and by no means stupid, and what affections still survived in her heart were given to Dick. Patsey was not the first young woman she had had reason to expect to have as a daughter-in-law, but she had realised from his letters that her son's feelings were now in an acute state and she thought from the anxiety he betrayed that this affair had gone deeper than those that she had hitherto watched both coming and going.

She had just seen Patsey once or twice in a crowd in London, but, with a common modernism, talked as if they had been very, very often together. Of course Mrs. Milward knew how to travel, and Patsey admired, besides the facilities of wealth, a far greater degree of skill for comfort than dear Aunt Mary's. Lady Lavington had to be taken about and her things rescued constantly and tips applied to make up for accidents, whereas travelling with Mrs. Milward everything went of itself, everybody feeling bound apparently to be efficient, and that without much reward.

There are weeks, evenings, hours in our lives which enrich all the years that follow, in which we see richer glories of sunlight and more mellow depths in the shadows, and thereby we have gained a greater power of understanding what to look for and to love. Such was Patsey's first evening in Fiesole late in September. By then the rose trees, parched in the great heats, have revived and are giving roses of a richer autumn depth of colour. It is in the early autumn that Florentine gardens have a second and a richer spring. And from one of the most beautiful

M 177

of its gardens Patsey looked down on Florence and across the city and the Arno to San Miniato and the Certosa. She had not a first rate historical knowledge. Each dome, each bridge, each piazza was not alive for her, as it was for Gemma, with the glories and the tragedies—all the passions of the past. But yet she had enough knowledge of the town and its history and enough imagination to feel the great wonder of it and enough soul to be drunk with its beauty.

Dick arrived in time for dinner at half-past eight and it struck Patsey at once that he was different in his mother's company. He seemed anxious to say the right thing according to some standard of talk which she could not understand. But the most important part seemed to be the careful avoiding of anything that could possibly bore her. Plans for the coming days as to seeing Florence, but still more as to seeing people who were passing through Florence, took up their time. Dick himself, the important great young man of promise, was not considered at all it seemed to Patsey, and she herself only came in for occasional courteous reminders that she was not really forgotten. When the servants left them alone for dessert Mrs. Milward concluded the proofs of her magnificent digestion by eating peaches and drinking port.

" When does the Duce arrive ? "

" On Saturday morning and he leaves on Tuesday night."

" How about his coming up here ? "

Patsey coloured in her anxiety for the reply, while Dick turned a deep red.

" I hope that's going to be all right, he drove out here last time he came to Florence, he likes the view."

" The least he can do for you after the way you have devoted yourself to him is to pay some attention to your mother." The words " your mother " sounded more combative than sentimental.

Dick at the same moment catching Patsey's eye telegraphed the information that it would be for somebody else's sake that he would bring the Duce, if it were humanly possible. Mrs. Milward soon after dinner got under weigh with her writing case and her fountain pen, and nodded her consent when Dick said that he and Patsey would go out.

His first remark was not one of enthusiasm at the sight of Florence lying in the moonlight :

" The devil's in it," he said. " Here's my mother going to be furious if the Duce does not come up here and not only is he likely to refuse but I doubt if she will see him at all. You see I have kept my promise and I am sure he will make time to see you. I got him interested about the death in the train, but that's the very limit of what I can do."

Patsey gave him a delighted smile that would have filled him with joy had he been less deeply worried.

" Has your mother anything special to say to him? "

" You don't understand," groaned Dick. " It is simply that for her to be in Florence and not see him seems to her an impossibility. She could never contemplate such a thing for a moment. She always does see anybody that really matters and to leave Italy not having seen Mussolini is what she won't do."

" But you can't force him ! "

" No, but all the blame will be for me."

" I'm so sorry."

" Oh don't be sorry, Patsey. I would not have told you, only I had to warn you. You must not appear to expect to see him at all, and it may have to be done under the rose."

Patsey felt that it was not for her to suggest that Mrs. Milward might get over her disappointment in time. By a day or two later she got so far into the Milward atmosphere that she shared Dick's sense of an immense catastrophe hanging over their heads.

Meanwhile nothing could have surpassed the skill and tact with which Mrs. Milward prepared her feast for the Dictator—for skill as to the material side and tact as to the servants belonging to the house were both needed. Then the choice of guests and the careless suggestion that the Duce might or might not come—probably he would not have the time to spare.

For a couple of days after this the road to the villa was positively crawling, not only with born toadies or chronic toadies, but with some very pleasant people turned toady by the presence of Mrs. Milward holding out the possibility of the great man's coming. If she had been only very beautiful or a great genuis or merely immensely rich her power would never have been what it was. The fact was that her popularity was soundly based on enormous wealth used with tact, energy and capacity. At the same time, if she had wished it, she could not have disguised the vitality of a tremendous will and the suggestion of an awful temper. From these qualities combined there resulted the social and domestic power of Dick's mother.

Patsey began to feel that if Mussolini came to the villa he would meet his match.

Patsey could not have seen Florence under better auspices, for of course everything was done that could be done to show all that was most wonderful to Mrs. Milward. Dick cursed the whole show in his poor worried mind, for he could hardly see anything of Patsey in his mother's crowd. It was a relief that the latter was occupied, for although he knew that she never for one moment lost her hold on her real objective, there were none of the harsh words or bursts of temper that he had first learnt to dread in his early childhood.

Patsey felt very sorry for him in the moments when she could think of anything but Mussolini or Florence. She thought him more handsome without so much self-confidence as he usually showed, also the increasingly large black rims round his eyes denoting sleeplessness gave them more depth. People in Florence spoke very well of Dick Milward and of the way in which he understood the situation in Italy. Several people told his mother that her son had great influence with Mussolini, and then Patsey fancied that her well formed lips closed more tightly.

THE SHADOW OF MUSSOLINI

The Duce arrived on Saturday and the villa seethed with rumours, while Mrs. Milward spent any intervals between visitors in studying large communications from London as to her stocks and shares. After dinner Dick drove up the long steep roads at a terrific pace and met Patsey, who was undisguisedly looking out for him.

" I haven't the ghost of a notion what is going to happen," he said. " He hasn't so much as recognised my existence. He has been at work ever since he arrived—except for the hour he spent at the Review he hasn't left his writing table, and nobody knows what meals he will have or when he will have them. He sends for all sorts of people big and little, and most of the big ones come out looking very small indeed, and the little ones look full of enthusiasm. There is no sort of official or editor in the whole place who feels safe. The English and American colony is alarmed because he won't allow foreigners to buy villas here, and he will make the Italians live in their own houses whether they like it or not. Nobody knows what will come next when he is on the warpath. Then I believe he's in an anti-luxury frame of mind, so if he comes here he will tell my mother what he thinks of her food. But I wish to heaven he would come ! What I'm afraid of is that some one will tell him that my mother owns an important newspaper and that's quite enough to send him off the deep end ! By the way who's here ? "

Patsey gave him three names, one the English ex-

BETTER TO BE AN ORPHAN

Prime Minister, one an Italian prince and one a great Italian playwright.

" Then it is to be hoped she won't have any time to spare for me."

" I'm afraid she wants you," said Patsey sympathetically—better to be an orphan like herself than to have such a parent living !

" It must seem absurd to you," he said, " but I grew up in it. My mother is a great woman. It's the only moral fear I've known until—until—you will laugh—until I saw the Duce—but it seems more natural with a man."

" And now the fears clash and I am the cause of the mischief—no ! not me I suppose, but the people who threaten him."

He gave her an affectionate smile :

" Are you really still full of that threat ? Do you seriously mean to tell the Duce himself ? "

Patsey stared. " Dick, do you think I'm an absolute humbug ? Do you really think that I am giving you all this trouble just because I want so badly to see Mussolini ? Oh dear, oh dear, what you must think of me ! "

" I think you," said Dick, " the most perfect——"

Patsey interrupted : " No, don't cover it up, my dear, it's just that you think all women are like that."

" I wasn't trying to cover up anything, Patsey, and I would do twice as much to gratify any whim of yours. I wish I could."

" So it's a whim," sighed Patsey. " But I know

it's all the kinder of you, and I'm not really ungrateful! Oh! I do hope I shan't be doing you any harm! Oh tell me I'm not!"

He looked big and kind and strong as he smiled ruefully: "Honestly I don't know. I seem to be between the devil and the deep sea at the moment. But I would willingly dare them both if I could get what I want! Patsey, shall I ever get what I want? No, don't tell me now, don't put the heart out of me. Come in. I'll see the mother while people are with her. Lord! how like the days when I was a small boy! Queer thing human nature——"

Patsey was saved again, but if he had forced it then what might she not have said.

CHAPTER II

Mussolini in Florence

SUNDAY night found Patsey waiting for the sound of Dick's car. He jumped out and joined her without seeing that there were no lights in the villa.

" How has mother taken it ? "

" Your mother has gone ! She went an hour ago."

" Good Lord ! And are you here alone ? "

" Yes, but I have taken a room at a convent in Florence, and I thought you would drive me down."

" Was she furious ? "

" Poor Dick, she didn't say much, but I never felt such an atmosphere. Lord R—— has gone with her. They sort of shook the dust of Florence off their feet and departed for a worthier city."

" But the Duce said he would see Lord R—— to-morrow."

" I suppose that was why he was removed. Am I very white, Dick ? The servants are all shaky."

" I am sorry, Patsey. I planned to make you so happy and you have been treated——"

" I haven't been treated badly exactly—I could have gone in the motor, at least I was told so by one of the servants as a message. Can we come away now, and do you think me silly, but I want to take the head man—what is his name—Pietro—down into Florence and let him see you deposit me at the convent. We ought to be off, they shut their gates at nine. But have you had any dinner ? "

" Damn dinner—I'll get something later. I must put you wise on one or two points to prepare you for to-morrow as we drive down into Florence."

Patsey could hardly have said afterwards whether the convent had been comfortable. She did not sleep, but that was probably not the fault of the bed. She drank a great deal of coffee in the morning, but that was more from the need of support than from the excellence of the coffee.

She unpacked her boxes, hunting for her best things, and then kept changing her mind as to which was most suitable to the occasion ; finally she wisely chose what suited her best. In the morning light, and in a different house with no connection with the villa, she was recovering her sense of proportion. Mrs. Milward had simply been in a very bad temper and she had an extraordinary amount of temper ! The woman had a very strong personality, developed by the submission of others and very rarely thwarted by fate and the laws of nature. Patsey knew no details of her history, but she had heard that those were the main lines of growth, and she had seen the results.

After this, if she ever saw Mrs. Milward again, she would feel the enormous savage vitality under the civilised exterior—and she would shake her hand if it were extended to her as she would accept the paw of a caged lioness. But with the return to common-sense an idea struck her for the first time—or rather she remembered words that now had a great deal of meaning. Some one in Geneva had said that Dick was rich, but that his mother was enormously rich, with a personal gift for finance, and had added, " But it's all in her own hands." Now Dick had—for Patsey's sake—risked and incurred his mother's extreme displeasure by obtaining an audience with the Duce for Patsey instead of for his mother. It was an uncomfortable thought intruding into her preparations for the event of the day. The day was long, hot and noisy. Patsey could neither read nor rest, either before or after *déjeuner*. She could not see further than the convent gate over which she saw pass a banner or two, and she heard, all through the long hours, the Fascists singing, while at moments there was loud cheering.

At about six o'clock Patsey, longing for tea but fearing to be missed if she went out to get it, was called to the parlour. She was perfectly ready.

Dick standing in the bare little room looked as solemn as Patsey felt. " He will see you now—I have a motor waiting."

As they came out a blackshirt was standing by the gate and after they had got into the motor he took his seat by the chauffeur. It was apparently owing to his presence that they passed very rapidly through the crowded streets.

Patsey looked half dazed as she passed through the

great hall of the Signoria and up the wide stairs.
Dick walked by her in silence, until at last he muttered, " Don't mind if he thinks you are my *fiancée*,
I could not help it," a remark that was not reassuring.
But she was by now so entirely wrapped up in her
mission, in the delivery of her message, that she was
not receptive to any other idea.

As they came into the fourth and last great room
in that suite, Patsey realised that she was face to face
with the Duce. He was sitting at a table and then
rose and bowed to her and told Dick to give her a
chair, adding that he need not wait. He did not
smile, nor did he look ungracious. Patsey's first
feeling was the sense of the racial barrier, which
almost overwhelmed her, it was so strong. And the
second was the absolute necessity of justifying her
own presence, under the glance of those overpowering
eyes. She stammered a little as she began and then
to her surprise found her self-confidence in the consciousness that he did not think her a fool. She told
him all she knew, and more than she had intended
to tell him as to Gemma and as to the death in the
train.

He asked questions at intervals, and only once he
smiled and that was when Patsey told him of the
wicked woman's last words. " She had personality,"
he commented.

Then when Patsey told him about her meetings
with Gemma at the café and at the Cathedral, he
made a note with a pencil on a pad. What astonished
her was that she was able to tell him more about

Gemma than she had been conscious of knowing until that moment.

"Then all the Signora Gemma asks is to be alone with me for the first and the last time, and the question is whether that is compatible with the safety of Italy." He looked over the table covered with papers and took up a number fastened together that were typed and annotated.

"These are the reports I have received concerning the Signora. I asked for them recently because she had been with the Russian whom you saw die in the train." He turned over two sheets, glancing rapidly down them. "Here, this is what we want." He looked across at Patsey. "These first sheets say how she left Campo, fearing—without cause—that she would be stopped at the frontier. At Lucerne station she was recognised by one of the police force, and he followed her to the Pension Victoria. This Pension is ostentatiously mysterious, and intended to divert the attention from the real Bolshevik *rendez-vous*. There has lately been a sale of furniture there, for some purpose unknown."

He read off each page detached sentences, passing quickly to the next. "Ah, here it is! 'We have a woman called Alexia at the Victoria, she has the drug weakness but is reliable. She says that she was sent with the Italian lady and carried her luggage. She was told to take her to the house in Lucerne where the great lady was very ill. The "great little lady" is the nickname known to your Excellency.'" The Duce's voice paused for a moment as he moved an impatient finger down the sheet. " In short," he went on looking at Patsey, " Gemma was taken straight, and quite willingly, to the little monster who was very ill and she at once began to nurse her and did her a world of good. Alexia, the spy, cleaned the rooms at Gemma's orders. You may be sure they wanted it. I can remember the monster's rooms." He gave a little chuckle which startled Patsey. "And she could hear them talking—arguing day and night. The monster was furious because Gemma went to church. She would be," he laughed. Patsey was too intensely anxious to realise that the Duce had a certain reminiscent interest in these details as to his one-time friend—the little monster. " Alexia deposes that one night Gemma went out soon after dark while she was left to wait on the patient, and she was frightened at the little monster's face. She had refused to sleep and had been fearfully excited. Alexia knew something had happened.

" The Signora returned in the small hours and Alexia listened secretly to their talk. She heard the Italian tell the Russian that she—Gemma—had been chosen to do the deed, and the great lady—or the little monster—was so pleased that she seemed quite well."

Patsey's anxiety rose above her fear of interrupting him. " But what deed ? " she cried.

The Duce raised his head and his great eyes looked straight into hers and beyond hers into depths she could not fathom—he smiled.

" The deed with them and with so many others means assassination."

" Not you ? "

" Yes, me, of course. But I must get through this stuff. The monster drank my health in vodhka, Alexia did not know if Gemma drank—she was very quiet while the patient was noisy—there seemed to be no disagreement.

" After that night Gemma was out oftener and was at all the meetings of the Bolsheviks in Lucerne. She was let go where she liked and let see whom she liked. She saw her friends at Basel, where she went one day with the monster, the latter in high spirits. Let me see, is that all that will interest you ? " He read on to himself for a few moments, while Patsey's heart sank and her breathing was difficult. She felt overcome by the sense of her own futility. Here she had come wholly ignorant of what had really happened, but the bubble of her supposed mission was burst. She was like a little self-important mouse playing in a futile way at the feet of a lion. At this moment even disappointment was nothing compared to the overwhelming desire that this man should not suffer. And yet could it—could it possibly be true of Gemma ? And there intruded the thought of Gemma in the Cathedral and the look on her face then—she knew that Gemma had looked ashamed, that she had been ashamed. And she, Patsey, if all this were true, had been trying to help Gemma to get at the Duce. She felt as if she were going crazy.

Presently the voice, even more cool and business-like, went on. " Gemma was sent to Geneva to see you, to help to trace the jewels." He paused. " I think that is all in this budget that is of interest." He put the papers aside and then spoke—more to himself than to her.

" This, Signorina, is all for your private information. I judge that you are able to keep a secret. Well then, keep this one. But you may wish to hear my own opinion, both of what you have told me and of the police report. Not to put it too politely, you certainly appear to have been a ' catspaw ' in the hands of a conspirator, coming in all good faith to me, but actually working out her designs. That is what appears on the surface and that is the opinion of the police, but—I trust my own psychology more than theirs—I consider all that to be merely on the surface. Until I gave you a fright you were not merely a messenger, you were also a most valuable witness. You have convinced me that your own first impressions were the true ones. Now you are confused and your second thoughts—as is so often the case—are not your best.

" I have decided to see the Signora, but on my own conditions. She must come to Italy under police escort and be kept under surveillance wherever I decide to put her. While I am out of Italy she will remain under the same conditions, and when I return she will be banished." He got up as he spoke. " I must not detain you longer. I will make one exception to the strict privacy I have enjoined. You will need an outlet. You may confide in your *fiancé.*" He pressed the bell on the table as he spoke. " I have every confidence in his discretion." In answer to his summons Dick appeared at one door and two Fascists at the other. They found the Duce and Patsey standing opposite to each other. The bow with which he finally dismissed her was much lower than the bow with which he greeted her. Then with the same tremendous Latin gravity he said—rather as a matter of business—two words in English, " Many thanks." Dick saluted, the Duce took no notice but sat down again and was consulting his notebook before they left the room, while the blackshirts waited for further orders.

" My goodness ! Patsey, he kept you twenty minutes and he took you quite seriously, I could see that."

But to his amazement Patsey began to cry even while they were walking through the crowd in the ante-rooms and on the stairs. " Do dry up, Patsey," he whispered, " for Heaven's sake. They have all been wondering at his keeping you so long, they will think you have been making love to him."

An effort at control threw Patsey into the other extreme and she was laughing uncontrollably as he hurried out into the air, and almost lifted her into the motor.

CHAPTER III

SUCH FORGIVENESS

DICK MILWARD showed some knowledge of nerves and their treatment in completely changing the subject of conversation. Also it was necessary to be practical, for nothing had been decided as to Patsey's next movement. Indeed no other thought beyond the audience vouchsafed by the Dictator had been in either of their minds.

He now spoke with marked firmness and authority. " In to-day's excitement I quite forgot to give you this note or to explain it. My mother came to her senses, it seems, early this morning and she telephoned to Mrs. Martin—you know the little woman with fuzzy dyed hair, quite a good sort. She asked her to stay at the villa with you until she could go with you to Geneva. Mrs. Martin is going to France and my mother thought it the best plan. She is up at the villa now so I think we had better drive up there at once if you don't mind, and settle what you like with her."

Patsey in a low uncertain voice made him understand that she agreed. During the rest of the drive they said little. Patsey felt vaguely grateful, and the sweet evening air and the sense of escape from Florence, with its overwhelming possibilities and meanings, did her good. A road with green trees hanging over white walls and a bunch of dusky red roses from time to time was dull but soothing.

" That means he is off to Milan," explained Dick after a long silence. But Patsey had not noticed the salute of guns enough to be curious. Now she felt as if it were all part of a dream about the man she had just left. He had gone, and in her exhaustion it was almost a relief.

Dick meanwhile chafed a little at having missed the farewell at the station. He knew so well those enthusiastic crowds, always with a core of adoring Fascists, disciplined apparently even in their worship of their Duce. . . . And the pride in them, the enthusiasm for them, the veneration for their obedience that the Dictator knew how to feel and to show them with few words. " My words are deeds," he had said once, in excusing his own brevity. His comrades, that was what his henchmen knew themselves to be, and he had once called Dick his English comrade. Dick watching the fair faint face of his love would not for the world have left her in any other keeping, but he would have liked to have been at the station.

Mrs. Martin received them at the villa with evident gusto for the situation. She was not sorry Mrs. Milward had told her not to let even Dick know that she was to have all her expenses paid first class, all the way to England. She was devoted to Mrs. Milward and felt how badly Dick had behaved in preferring his lady love to his mother. That a mere

195

chit of a girl should have seen Mussolini, while his mother—with her vast influence and great gifts—was scorned and ignored was really shocking. All the Florence that knew Mrs. Milward at all had got wind of the catastrophe and was indignant. Mrs. Martin felt these young people to be culprits and thought with satisfaction that Patsey looked distinctly ashamed. But the softer parts of her heart yielded some sympathy to the lovers, and the tone of his voice when Dick asked for immediate food and drink for Patsey stirred her with a touch of memory's sweet pain, for Mr. Martin had always wanted her to take something when she felt faint.

Dick was not sorry that the major-domo had seen Patsey deposited at the convent the evening before— it seemed to save her dignity now. His first thought was that Patsey and Mrs. Martin might well have a few days at the villa, but he found that they both wanted to get off at once and he had no sufficient argument for keeping them. All Mrs. Milward's Florence would know that Mrs. Martin was travelling with Patsey, and he himself had better see if he got any informal kind of orders from the Duce. What he hoped for was that the great man might suggest that he could again be useful at Geneva.

It was not until next morning that he saw Patsey without Mrs. Martin, that kind woman having insisted on repacking Patsey's box that had been brought up from the convent in a state of dire confusion.

They went out into the garden together, and then,

to his astonishment, Patsey quietly and with entire self-command told him the whole story of Gemma.

Dick listened in amazement, he had formed some vague notion that Patsey had perhaps " dreams and omens and such like fooleries " by which to warn the Duce. Or, when taking the famous warning more seriously, he had supposed that the dwarf in her last moments had revealed some evidence of a plot. When the Duce gave twenty precious minutes to listen to Patsey and thanked her in that business-like fashion he had been surprised and impressed. But Patsey's story of Gemma—and of Rodney Castle incidentally—took him entirely by surprise. Since the great interview, Patsey herself saw it all from a different point of view. Now Mussolini dominated the whole, not Gemma nor Castle—who came in simply as a necessary factor in the story. Now her one thought seemed to be for the Duce.

" Here have I been playing round fancying myself as very important because I had got news for the Duce—and he knew every movement Gemma had made ! He even knew about me ! And now I don't know what to think—I feel half crazy. I do believe in Gemma, but just—just suppose I'm wrong. Supposing—for one ought to suppose everything— that she has used me as a means of getting at him— supposing she killed him after all ! "

Then to her astonishment Dick laughed : " Patsey, Patsey he has gone to your head and I'm not surprised. How could she possibly hurt him ? She will be brought here as you say by his people. Don't

197

you see that she will be a prisoner at the Duce's pleasure, that she can be searched until she could not conceal the smallest implement or the tiniest dose of anything ? If she agrees to come he is taking the Bolshevist pawn prisoner, if she does not agree she is a marked woman easily avoided. It is a wise gesture too and they will all admire his magnanimity and shudder at his rashness. He is the bravest thing alive, but of course they never choose the right things to admire him for. Patsey, do you suppose your Gemma will really walk into the lion's mouth ? "

"Of course I do, because I believe in Gemma. Then really and truly Dick, you don't think my meddling has done any harm ? " She wanted more reassuring.

"Harm ? No. You have given him a capital opportunity, for either he will take the pawn or she may really have something important to tell him. There's just a third possibility, Patsey. Just suppose that from the wild hatred and delusion of these people she really meant to kill him, or that she has been terrorised into agreeing, she may have repented and thinks this the way of escape. It's frightfully interesting. I wonder when we shall know."

They discussed it all over again and then another point struck Dick.

"What made you get so keen about Gemma from the very beginning ? "

"Oh! Rodney Castle's story took my fancy and I wanted to help him."

"Why to help him ? "

SUCH FORGIVENESS

"Well, because he was in love and he is a friend of mine."

There was something in the way she said those words that increased his anxiety.

"A great friend, Patsey?"

"Yes, Dick."

"And you were determined not to be jealous?"

Patsey flushed and was silent.

"You have been very generous, Patsey, but have you been quite just?"

Patsey made an indignant gesture and then felt that she was defenceless. "I would have told you," she cried, "only I could not bear to own it when it was no use and——"

"I would have done anything for you Patsey anyhow. I don't want to grumble—only it would have been kinder don't you think?"

"I thought I made it clear that I could never be more to you than a friend and I thought I should get over the other nonsense."

"And have you got over it?"

He was very angry—but oh! so ready to turn from wrath to tenderness. Patsey looked straight in front of her.

"I am afraid not."

There was silence after that, an awful silence. Everything seemed to ooze out of Patsey as she sat there, she had not even tears to shed; pride and hope and the sense of adventure—even the sense of her pitiful affection for Rodney Castle—all melted away as if in an enormous moral sweat.

" I think you ought to be getting ready, the motor has come."

Dick stood up. During the hurry of the next ten minutes he did not speak to her again. He was busy having last words with Mrs. Martin and giving directions to the villa servants. Also in adding his own tips to those his mother had deputed to the happy Mrs. Martin to distribute.

" Are you staying on at the villa ? " Patsey heard Mrs. Martin ask him as they stood in the hall.

" No," he said, " I believe I shall go to Milan for the manœuvres."

Then just as the servants were busy fastening the trunks behind the motor and Mrs. Martin was looking in the drawing-room for her wrist-bag, fat with unwonted pelf, Dick and Patsey were alone.

" I'm glad you saw him, Patsey."

She understood what that meant to him, but such forgiveness left her speechless.

CHAPTER IV

DROPPED BY THE DUCE

DICK had meant to see Patsey off at the station, but he did not go beyond the hall of the villa and he allowed the old Italian servant to do all that was to be done at the last moment.

Then as the motor turned a little on the drive he turned back into the house without a last look, without knowing if there were any farewell waved towards him.

He nursed his wrath, while he told himself that he was too busy for any sadness to get the better of him. He was very impatient to be gone and was relieved to find how efficient and complete had been his mother's orders to Mrs. Martin and to the upper servants. In fact nothing had been left for him to do and he was free. What he hoped for was some immediate direction from the Duce himself to follow him to Milan. To be near his hero, to watch his genius at work forming the rising Italy out of old elements and new, inspiring young hearts with the traditions of antiquity, inducing a spirit of sacrifice in old and young. It was a complete reaction from materialism yet it did not ignore facts; it was an idealism that built bridges and cleansed unhealthy dwellings with fresh waters and lit up the darkness of the streets where vice had gone hidden and un-punished. To Dick—the child of a woman who was the very type that money and capacity produce, with its profound cynicism of anything not built on gold and its all embracing self-indulgence in art, in music, even in the spiritual life—to Dick, the Duce had been a personal liberator. He had not got beyond the stage of idealism, and his mind was too sound to wish for foolish propagandism or imitation. Fascism in England would never appeal to him.

He had sent for a motor and was walking up and down the short drive trying not to think of Patsey, trying not to worry about his mother's power of punishing the wrongdoer, when a blackshirt jumped off a motor bike at the gate. He was little more than a child, but he led his bike with his left hand until he was close to Dick, when he proudly gave the Fascist salute and drew a letter out of his wallet. Dick tore it open and flushed with pleasure when he saw the Duce's signature in his own writing. The boy instantly turned round, and was flying down the hill before Dick realised that he had gone.

The letter was typewritten in Italian. At first Dick tried to believe he was mistaken in its meaning, then he looked round for some place where no curious eyes could see him, and with a sick heart walked across the garden to the same bench where he had sat while Patsey had struck the blow that was the first of that day's sorrows.

He spread it out and bent over it. Yes, it was dis-missal, dismissal from voluntary loyal hero-service.

DROPPED BY THE DUCE

And why ? Why, because Dick's mother owned a
newspaper, and he would never be on terms with the
bought press beyond the Alps. Dick's silence had
been mere ignorance, and the Duce would ever
remember his first young English comrade, a comrade inspired with Fascist ideals, with hatred for
vices masquerading under platitudes. As a farewell
word of advice he assured him that those ideals could
never live in his soul unless he guarded it from the
sinister influence of materialism. He wished him
well and congratulated him on his *fiancée*, who was
noble and frank and loyal, and to her also he extended his congratulations, for each was as fortunate
as the other.

When Patsey had struck, Dick had had her presence as a motive for control. When the Duce struck,
he was alone. Wrath, the eternal wrath of man
rejected by woman, had, in spite of the anguish of the
heart, seemed almost to strengthen him—a surging
of disgust against his hero had not the same power.
He seemed to see the Duce cutting him away in a
favourite gesture, a gesture to make an impression.
Mussolini knew perfectly well that he, Dick, had had
no motive, no object in his service for Fascism that
was not single-hearted. Yet he felt convinced that
in order to prevent the faintest suspicion that he had
about him the son of a newspaper potentate he had
cast him off without the faintest regret. The bubble
of his poor self-esteem, which had been harmless,

honest, undisguised, was badly pricked. People, he knew (the young mostly do know what is thought of them), people had thought him too obviously prosperous, too well gifted, too conscious of his gifts.

However the very faults of self-confidence and artless satisfaction with his lot had not been those of a weak character. Dick was a strong man, and though Tennyson was quite wrong in saying that a man of strong will does not suffer long, he was nearer the truth in saying that he will not suffer wrong.

BOOK V

CHAPTER I

After the First Exile

If we in the North who mourn the loss of our brief summer and have reason to dread the advance guard of the menacing winter yet love the autumn, how much more must it be loved by those who rejoice in their escape from the great heat of a too long summer.

It was a glorious autumn night on which Gemma came back to her own land.

An elderly Fascist, for there are such, who was sitting by her side in the motor, looked up at the fomidable gateway and gave a brief order to a young man who sat next the chauffeur. The cracked bell sounded harsh, but, unlike most convent bells, it was instantly obeyed and a lay sister opened the door. The Fascist saluted her and she stood silent and expectant until Gemma was within the doorway. The three men did not salute their charge, but they bowed as she passed between them. The chauffeur handed a suitcase and a basket to the lay sister, and the door was shut. The Fascists prepared to spend the rest of the night outside the gate. The moon had disappeared and the stars were very great in the dark blue heavens—each star suggesting and withholding some secret that we cannot bear as yet.

The astonished lay sister had had orders to break

every minor rule that night, and holy obedience was severely strained, for the constitution of an order represents the rights of the subject.

Inside the convent was a further enclosure guarding the nuns from even the contact with the world that passed its business through the lay sisters.

For this Gemma was prepared, for she knew she was to be sent to an enclosed convent, but she was surprised at finding that she was to pass into the enclosure in the middle of the night. The heavily studded door leading into the walled garden creaked on its hinges, and a large figure, the face completely hidden by the veil, could be seen inside. The convent garden was full of life at rest, rich with the sounds that make up what we call silence, while the air was laden with almost unutterable sweetness.

Then Gemma, having taken her things from the lay sister, stepped over the threshold of this secret world, and it seemed to her that after an age-long journey the flowers and fruits sung of in the canticle of spiritual secrets were waiting for her, and their sweetness held her up. The silent nun led her round to the garden door nearest the cells, and then turned into one where a little oil lamp with a tiny flame burning on a float was dull in the starlight. Then she said, " *Avanti*—come in, Signora. I hope all will be well with you here."

The silence of the place seemed to have cast a spell over Gemma. She stood there travel-stained, weary, worn out by what was past, by what she had seen and heard, things undreamed of in the other

woman's knowledge of life. Then as her eyes fell
on the narrow bed, the spotless sheets, the white walls,
the stars through the window high above her, she saw
in the corner the little lamp before a picture of the
Madonna of Good Counsel—that ancient devotion.
It is a very early, primitive picture in which the
Babe is whispering words of good counsel to His
Mother.

She covered her face with her hands, and tears
trickled through her fingers. The Prioress was never
hurried and now she was enormously, painfully interested in this mysterious prisoner or guest. One
thing only she was sure of, it would be wrong to
intrude—a busybody with souls she detested. Her
order was the most individualist in the Church.
When the Bishop had said, " I shall be glad if you
will do what the Duce asks," she had wanted to
know if the prisoner herself was willing. When the
Bishop had said he would put great value on the
Prioress's judgment in this strange case, she had said
nothing. She was not at all sure she would be able
to judge ; she certainly would not pry and if she
came to a conclusion, well, short of the duty of
obedience, she would probably keep her opinion to
herself.

She did not ask anything about those tears, she
saw only that Gemma needed much rest and must
take it. She stood silent, not knowing that she made
Gemma feel the sense of the Presence in which they
had met ; after a few moments she offered food with
the little air of triumph that showed that food in

o   209

the night was a bold thought, but Gemma had dined in the train.

In her sweet detached voice, the voice of a woman still young, her " *Buona notte* " sounded like a little lost blessing floating in the air and then she went away.

Gemma still stood looking at the stars, overwhelmed. So much there was to feel and to suffer in this homecoming to her native land as a prisoner, as one suspected, by some already condemned. Yet what overwhelmed her was the sense of peace. Presently she could hear voices singing in the chapel, distant and monotonous—but they seemed to her part of a great and clear joy of the soul. She sat down on the one hard chair and listened. Then she rose and washed in the very small basin and went through the unpacking of her few clothes. And all through the time taken by these small tasks and while she lay sleepless on the hard narrow bed, she smiled. There was little outward difference between this cell and that of a prison, and Gemma was a prisoner. Whatever might come after to-night, she was as willing a prisoner as those nuns who were praising God—who were His prisoners—not Mussolini's.

It would be impossible to anyone who did not know what she had suffered to guess the midnight joy of the woman whose weary figure had aged three years in the course of as many months. But she was not less striking from being a little older. It mattered to nobody the grandeur of the figure as she lay with her eyes wide awake, large, watchful and beautiful. She had slept very little lately, but she was not impatient of the hours of the night like a good healthy sleeper lying awake. Gemma tried not to think, tried not to rehearse over and over and over again what she had come to say to " the tyrant "—not to rehearse, not to make decisions. Without supposing herself to be acting under inspiration she felt a great trust that it would be given her what to say.

Another weary work of the undistracted imagination in the watches of the night was to go over again each horror of the last few months. " It is past ! It is past ! " she kept saying to herself, and to-night she could feel that the sordid life in which she had mixed, with its stink of sin affecting the most harmless actions, its cruelty blackening courage and its lust corrupting love, all this was left behind.

And then she remembered that this convent, this prison of peace, but of suffering, held lives that were offered in expiation precisely as a sacrifice for those among whom she had herself been thrown. There was no indifference here—to the worst, the vilest of the underworld, nothing but love and mercy. Some few minutes' sleep she did get towards five o'clock, not long, but long enough to know what it was to wake there and then.

She woke with a start feeling none of the things she had felt in the night, only in the grip of another idea, of dread and half of shame.

What did the nuns think about her ? What had

they been told ? Was she allowed in their secret precincts as one who had fallen into the depths, or as an honoured guest ? Why had the tyrant chosen this most rigid of convents, and why had the Bishop agreed to the choice ? Gemma knew enough of convent rules to know that something very special had been done before this had been possible.

However the first trouble of waking, the first serious sense of being in a possibly unfriendly climate, passed away as she knelt in the chapel. He Who knew the worst of her gave her a Divine welcome that morning.

CHAPTER II

FACE TO FACE

THE man who had been transformed from a journalist
to an autocrat certainly had the hero-worship which
it is said that valets do not give. The police were in
deadly earnest in their measures of defence, and there
is probably among all the nerve racking careers of
the present day few more nerve racking than that
of the police. The doctors appointed for the London
police insist on short service, and it is one of their
preoccupations to look out for the nightmares that
are the first symptoms of a policeman's overstrain.
But given the peculiar conditions of Italy at the
moment and it may be imagined that the police
appointed to safeguard the person of Signor Mussolini
had troubled slumbers.

Rarely has any man provoked so many schemes
of assassination as he, for not only had he defied and
defeated the forces of the red revolution, but he had
upset the plans and hopes of all those who fish in
troubled waters. Even some of those whose schemes
had been within the law had to submit to the unpleasant fact that these plans were now without it.
Among other things it was said that when he shut
the Casinos in the Italian Riviera, on which col-
ossal fortunes had been spent, he had aroused the

antagonism of reckless men. So that between the Bolshevists of the deeper dye, the Freemasons whom he had withstood throughout, the men whose vicious or merely avaricious schemes he had destroyed, and the lunatics or semi-lunatics whose mad imaginations always fasten on the great man of their day, there were very many ready to make away with him. But what excited the police to fever pitch was the coolness of the central figure. " One never knows what he will do next," they said. If he had shown any anxiety about himself, made even any enquiry about their precautions, he would have roused less zeal. As it was, they were always ready in his own words to do " a little more than was possible " in his service. It was up to them to keep him alive and thereby to save themselves. Did he, perhaps, with his incomparable psychology, know that nothing could have secured greater care of his person than his own absence of care in the matter ?

Those in command dared not even mutter their feelings when they knew the Duce intended to give an interview to Gemma. It was not that, like Patsey, they had any fear that Gemma guarded and searched could do him bodily harm, but they thought it a sheer folly to see the would-be murderer. It was not the way to inspire terror, it was not according to any procedure they had ever heard of. If information was to be got from her, there were other methods. Gossip as to Gemma was rife among the Fascist journalists, though it did not get into print as the discipline imposed on the press was already at that date severe.

All things just then tended to the glory of the Duce, as Dick Milward had foreseen, for loyal heads and hearts were positively wallowing in submission and admiration, so that any incident added fuel for incense.

Who was the murderess who was to be allowed to see the Duce face to face ? It was a question that a thousand guesses tried in vain to answer. Where was she to be kept ? Two prisons and two convents were asserted to have been chosen. At least two reverend mothers were pestered with enquiries and refused to see visitors, while heroically suppressing some natural curiosity on their own part. The Duce himself had decided that she should arrive late at night at a convent twenty miles out of the city.

He, too, chose the place of meeting, and that was not merely because it would be unlikely to be found out. Milan, the scene of his labours as a struggling editor, held many old haunts of his past life ; he had a large choice of inconspicuous houses. He chose the old office of the *Avanti*, now belonging to a group of Fascist newspapers, in which to see the lady about whom there might easily be too much fuss. It was the office in which in the early days of the war he had had visits from her *promesso sposo* who had come in those days from Florence to consult Benito Mussolini and work under his orders. Did he intend to recall that past link, to remind her that her own husband had been devoted to himself ?

THE SHADOW OF MUSSOLINI

The offices were now abandoned, but the Duce sometimes used the one large shed at the back for his pet exercise of fencing. He would see Gemma, when he had finished his brief recreation, in one of the disused rooms which opened into the shed. Such were the orders that sent blackshirts flying out to the convent to break into Gemma's new found peace. The Fascists and the regular police combined to bring the would-be assassin to her audience.

It looked what it was, the deserted office of a newspaper : an office that had had nothing of display in furniture or decoration.

Gemma sat alone in a large ricketty wooden chair, her hands clasping the arms. For the first time she had felt what it was to be in the hands of the police, literally to be handled by the searchers, who were powerful well-trained women. There had been little to distinguish the treatment from that of hospital nurses who were preparing patients for operation, except for the absolutely negative attitude of the searchers.

It was impossible it should not be an indignity, but the willing passivity of the central figure and the extreme reserve of the others diminished, at least, the outward effect of humiliation. To Gemma this seemed so little a thing compared to what was to come ; but once left alone to wait for the next act in the drama, she certainly felt that what had happened had left her on a lower plane on which to meet her fellow-men. The utter defencelessness of a human being, handled as she had been, must have some effect in increasing the awful sense of a desolate helplessness.

Gemma shivered, and then she set her teeth and turned her thoughts from all that was merely external. After a moment she began to pray, intent on gaining strength, on losing the weakness of a very human self. Presently she began to notice noises through the rough boarded wall and she at once recognised that somebody was fencing. The usual terms, the clash, the cries and the occasional applause were all familiar to her. Then she remembered hearing it said that the Duce still kept up his favourite pastime. Once that idea was in her mind she began to listen more attentively, and she fancied that one voice dominated the others while the weaker voices seemed servile in applause. "Detained during the king's pleasure," was a phrase that when used for the misery of a man's imprisonment had always offended her. Now after the indignity of the preparation to be allowed to enter Benito Mussolini's presence, she was to wait in agony and suspense while he took his pleasure. It was only half an hour, for in reality the Duce had very little time to spare, and it would be his only recreation that day, but to Gemma it appeared a very long hour.

"Patience, firmness," she muttered, as, with her face buried in her hands, she strove against the passionate resentment that threatened to be fatal to all action.

But when the Duce stood in front of her a great calmness succeeded the storm. No man was ever in more constant, unintermittent possession of the gifts needed for action, and of bringing the same to bear at any moment on the problem before him. They were both Italian of the Italians to the core of their being, and yet they could lose all sense of the molten lava of passion that was really within them in the overmastering intensity of urgent action.

With the man it was habitual to use his full strength for every detail of administration, every contact with men and women, much as a vast machine uses the same strength to crack a nut or a piece of granite. With the woman it was the sense of the crisis, the enormous issues that seemed to her to depend on what would come of the part she had to play.

The Duce had meant to speak to her of the man she mourned and the work they had done together in that room. But the moment he saw her he knew they must meet as having no links in the past, merely as having to settle a problem here and now.

Gemma rose and bowed, the Duce bowed and sat down. Her chair was in the corner by the dirty window and the light fell on her pale face on the left as she sat down. The Duce drew a chair up to the table and faced the light.

" You asked to see me," he said, but as she kept silent he went on—" As you know you are accused by both the Swiss and the Italian police of intending to assassinate me. My own view is that by consenting to come here on my conditions you go a long way to prove that these charges are false, or that before this you had changed your mind and no longer intended to kill me. But, given the facts as far as I know them, I think I am entitled to ask you for an explanation."

"Si, si!" said Gemma, and then in a low but firm voice she began. "You are of course right in your first suggestion. I never in my life thought of killing you or any one else. That," with a little smile, "has never been among my temptations. Apart from such a question, I had definitely cleared my life as a Christian of hatred of you, of ill-will, of revenge. But I have not come here of my free will merely to tell you that. I must describe to you all that happened to me in Lucerne." She paused.

After a few moments Mussolini came to her rescue; his voice and manner did not suggest sympathy, but the sense of solemn necessity of getting on with the business. "Some of it I know. You were persuaded to see a sick woman, you nursed her, you were tricked into attending a secret meeting at which lots were drawn, the lot, probably prearranged, fell on you. You then went back to the sick woman and told her that the doing of the deed was your fate, and what you told her was reported to the police."

"By the servant Alexia?" queried Gemma.

"Precisely."

"All that is true, and all that is what was intended to be known to the police," Gemma went on, "and from the first moment I had a most strong feeling that it was a got-up affair ready for the police to report to their own government and to you."

The Duce nodded gravely and very respectfully.

" It was all like a thing in a story book, the most childish means were used to impress me, but also to impress the spies who were there and who were known to be there, and who were so foolish as to fall into the trap. But I asked myself why on earth should the scoundrels trust me with their real plans ? To trust me with a false one, to make me take part in it from sheer terror, would discredit my friends quite enough and would save the risk of my knowing too much." She paused for a moment. " I need not justify to you, but to a higher power, my methods of deluding them. They were mostly passive. But I gained what I wanted to gain. They thought me simple, kindly, not too strong-minded. I don't think they trusted me, but they became accustomed to me and they were convinced that I was prepared to shoot you." A wan smile flitted over her face, followed by a groan. " I lived in hell, and I knew all the time that those I loved best were being discredited because I had disgraced myself. After that the Popolari, quite rightly, cut me off." For the first time the firm contralto notes were tremulous, but she seemed to gain control in a moment.

" I gained what I wanted, which was knowledge of what was the real plot, while I was only part of the camouflage. I found that the upper floors of five houses in Lausanne had been taken by five most respectable men and women, and cellars on two routes had been secured. There is no street you can possibly pass through from the station in which there is not some capital position of attack. But there was this degree of caution. I have no names, no proofs to give you. I tried to get you warned through an English acquaintance, he and a young lady whom I believe to be his *fiancée* could get no attention from their Foreign Office. At last I saw the young English lady herself, and she with a wonderful quickness knew what was to be done and came to you herself." She paused, and the Duce turned his chair to the old office table on which his first battles had been fought and spread out a large detailed map of Lausanne.

" The police in Lausanne are excellent."

" Si, Signor," answered Gemma. " But they are acting on false information. There has been very great astuteness with information ready for their spies who are very proud of having discovered their subtlest plots."

" Every street," murmured the Duce, " every street in which I wandered hungry seeking for a job," he smiled at her, " no one wanted to murder me then."

In her eagerness to convince him they seemed to have been almost friendly, but his personal allusion awoke other feelings and Gemma visibly stiffened. The Duce traced the different routes with a pencil in silence. " The police have put a danger mark on the first street we should have passed through," he observed.

" Probably," said Gemma scornfully, " that is the only safe one."

" Very likely." He slowly folded up the map. " There is something I don't understand."

" There are many things I do not understand," said Gemma coldly.

" I think you do understand the thing that I do not understand at this moment," said the Duce. " Why have you done so much to save me ? "

The enormous force of his valuation of himself was in the question, and the sense of it roused all her power of self-defence.

" Be content, Signor Mussolini, to know my actions, even here I suppose my thoughts may be my own."

" Even here," he replied, " one may be allowed to try to understand them."

Gemma folded her hands as if with infinite patience, with the stillness that in a Latin is a weather signal.

" A Christian forgives her enemy," he said, " and those of your party are real Christians."

" Also patriots ! " she exclaimed.

" It is patriotic then to save me ? " he asked in genuine surprise.

Gemma bent forward. " Will you ever understand ? " she exclaimed. " We don't wish to disturb your government. If all authority is to be in the hands of one man, we would rather it was yours than Lenin's. You have left us only a choice of servitudes. We will not talk of the past," she went on rapidly—for one moment she showed as much of the Imperial Latin as he did. " We will speak of the present, Signor. You are in power, a power we do not dispute; we think that your death at this moment would be a calamity to our country. I am here simply because I thought I saw a way to save Italy from the blow. Again, I knew that even if I escaped from your enemies and got quietly to England, you or yours would accuse the Popular Party of being in the plot when it burst. I saw a way to clear my party and to save you. More than that I will not say."

"Wonderful courage," he murmured to himself, with that enormous power of admiration for character that has been one of his chief assets as a leader. "I know the world you have been in. Heavens! for you to have been there! But let that pass. But if you do not wish my rule to be cut short, if you saw that I was the lesser of two evils, explain to me why from the outset the Popolari did not help me? Why, in the name of justice, not submit and live happily under my rule?"

Gemma's face was alight in a moment, and as she turned to the window her features were clearer to him than they had been till that moment.

"Submit, Duce! Live here tongue-tied slaves, we who have loved liberty and taught liberty, liberty from the tyranny of Bolshevism and also from every other tyranny? You, a journalist, who used liberty even to licence, you now command that no word shall be uttered that is not of servile adulation. Well then, we were to live here and swell the chorus of adulation! We were even to sit in your Chamber in order, as you say, to 'discuss *and approve*' the

223

measures you deign to put before us. We are to vote in municipal elections when there is only one candidate, and that a Fascist! It is not good enough, Benito Mussolini, for the children of the true *Risorgimento*. Better exile to a free country than——"
She suddenly stopped and covered her face with her hands. What is more bitter for a woman than to know that she has risked the fruit of past suffering from want of self-control? She had said she need not tell him more of her motives than she had done, and now she felt only the most powerful motive of all, the hope that if she could persuade this man of the *bona fides* of the Popular Party he would, on his side, be not only fair but generous.

The tears had not trickled through her fingers before she uncovered her face that showed the glory of courage through much pain.

"Ah!" she cried, "Signor Duce, you are a great man, and the great can afford to be magnanimous."
Mussolini looked straight at the window and did not break the silence that followed.

"Can you not see," she cried, "how much greater it would be to allow a rational liberty, how much safer it would be? I am not speaking of personal safety, but safety for carrying out your best ideals. Can you not see how you could build on a surer foundation than that of tyranny? Could you not find room in your plan of government for an honourable, upright, constitutional opposition, would you not be stronger and show confidence in your own power by doing so? Signore, I said I need not tell you all my motives for what I have done, but I will now. I came here believing you to be capable of generosity, the opinion of a loved one in the past made me hope. Seeing you now, I tell you with all candour, I believe you to be so great that I cannot think you will deliberately choose to be a tyrant. Think," she wailed with a great note of utterly unconscious tragedy, "think what a tyrant becomes. You do not fear now, perhaps you will never fear, bombs or pistol-shots, but you will live in a false atmosphere. You will be set about with flatterers, you will only hear what you wish to hear, you will have a more and more excessive sense of your own gifts. Ah, God! Signor, do you not fear moral littleness at all ? "

There she stopped as if she could, as was indeed the case, imagine no greater calamity. Nothing of what was said was new to him, but it was new as it came from her to him. He had been leaning forward a little. Now he sat upright and his eyes were fixed upon her.

" As long as I am the people's choice, as long as I have a work to do for them, as long as I make them play their part in the world, so long, Signora, I am not afraid of moral littleness ! I choose to be a tyrant, if to be a tyrant is to enforce submission to what is right, and to burn out of this people's lives all that is vile and corrupt. Has it ever struck you, Sig.aora, that people are perhaps tired of liberty ? I mean, of course, political liberty, the liberty to choose the wrong legislators, the liberty to be swayed by every

P

popular mood, the liberty to make sound government an impossibility, the liberty to live a life morally and physically unhealthy? You know perfectly well what Italy had come to "—then as she seemed about to interrupt, he raised a hand in command. " I know you will say that you were and would have been the saviours of the situation, but as a fact you did precisely fail to save it "—the hand, now so terribly powerful, warned her again.

" You split among yourselves, you started well but you could not go on, there was the hopeless weakness in your plan, the notion of decentralisation. To prevent over-centralisation in a healthy community may be good, but to decentralise in the midst of confusion is a counsel of despair. As a matter of fact you did *not* succeed, and I *have* succeeded and shall succeed. To you, probably, I owe the escape from the only thing that can prevent that success. I mean death. You won't accept thanks, I will not be impertinent enough to force them on you.

" You say that I should be big enough to allow opposition. I should be big enough if human nature were big enough. But I know the littleness of mankind ; I will not brook opposition, I will not do it for the sake of the adulation which, as you say, is probably a moral danger. I will not endanger Italy in order to appear magnanimous. Brutus was caught by the desire to appear magnanimous. He allowed Mark Antony to speak to the mob. That scene has never left my memory. I will not tolerate any

criticism whatever. The man at the wheel allows
no criticism from the passengers. I must do my job
and that alone. I can make you no return that you
would deign to accept for what you have done for me.

" I have overstayed my time here, Signora. I am
waited for even now." The Duce stood up.

" *Avanti*," he cried, and the door from the fencing
room was opened instantly.

Gemma rose.

" Signor, I must see you again."

" Such is my intention," he replied. He then gave
the Fascist salute and left her.

CHAPTER III

Thinking Aloud

Gemma had not to wait a moment before a Fascist officer, whom she had not seen before, came to ask her to have *déjeuner* with his wife in a house not far off. His manner was most respectful and cordial. Gemma felt at once that the negative attitude towards her would be changed. But that interested her little. Signs of the autocrat's favour were no longer of any value.

She very quietly but politely explained that she wished to get back to the convent at once, if that were allowed—the last words alone showed the proud humility that she could not hide, either in her bearing or in her glance. The man, who seemed to be a person of importance, took her to the motor and gave the inevitable Fascist salute as she was driven away.

All in vain, all lost, all spoilt, such were the thoughts that overpowered Gemma. At that moment the fact that the Duce had believed her story, and that she had, if he acted on her warning, saved his life, was almost lost sight of in the overpowering indignation at his last words.

" I can do nothing for you."

He accepted the saving of his life as a work done

for Italy, he was amazed at her courage, he exonerated her friends! But he hardened visibly at the bare mention of any generosity on his own part.

"I will not brook opposition or criticism. Anything of the kind will make me harder, more intolerant, more impossible." Such was his attitude now, an attitude that would but be more accentuated as the years passed. What was to happen to any country that gave itself, bound hand and foot, into such durance? "Gave itself!" No, it had not given itself, it had been tricked by a man who called himself a Liberator. "Liberatore, Liberatore," she muttered to herself with indescribable bitterness. The poor country had put the harness on its own neck and now it was being flattered by the prospect of riding over its enemies, of again taking a front place among the nations. The glory of Roman antiquity itself had been built on slavery! Must they be slaves again if they were to be among the world's masters? Gemma was exhausted. She could keep no order in her thoughts and fancies, all she could do was not to betray them as they surged over her.

Arrived at the convent after a drive that seemed endless, she had to wait for the eggs, cheese and wine that were at last brought to the parlour. The nuns had been told that she would lunch in Milan. The short meal finished, she was drinking coffee, unconsciously soothed by the utter peace of the garden seen through the widely opened windows.

Then a nun came in whom she had seen for a few

minutes on her first day in the convent. This sister was very tall, and had struck Gemma as being different from any nun hitherto known to her. She had found out she was a widow, an Englishwoman, whose four sons had been killed in the war—not boys, but grown men—and she was now far on in years, having lost her husband while her children were young. It was a clear, pallid face showing subtle traces of much experience, while the eyelids were a little red, as if the tears, no longer shed, still coloured the transparent lids. She was clearly a woman of the world, probably of the world that is often called 'great.' A large knowledge of life underlay the obvious spiritual peace that had come after more than common suffering.

"May I stay with you for a little?" she asked. And she accentuated her vowels in the Italian words a little wrongly. She was surprised and pleased when Gemma answered in English. They sat near each other facing the garden. For a few moments Gemma was tongue-tied, but she did not want to be left alone.

"Ah!" she said, harsh in the effort to speak at all, "this poor country, this poor Italy, how happy you are in England."

"It does not seem that we think ourselves very happy." The speaker crossed her arms in her sleeves so that the long exquisite hands were hidden and her thin shoulders gave a movement of mingled amusement and protest.

"Ah! but you have no tyrant!"

"We have several," cried the Englishwoman, "the press, the political machine, the——"

"Ah! but still you are free, not like us."

Then Gemma inevitably told her story, took the chance of this woman's listening. She told it all, amazed at herself as it poured out, she saw almost at once the deep interest, the fellow feeling, and gradually even the kindled enthusiasm in the face of the mother of many dolours.

It is a mistake to think that age and experience of the spiritual life check impulsiveness. The holy are so often aflame with impulses. The long taper fingers, still slightly marked where heavy rings had pressed, were laid on the young woman's arm.

"Ah, my dear! I don't know whether you have been wise, but you have been grand."

"You don't think I was wise, wise is precisely what I thought myself." Gemma smiled a little as she spoke. "It has not been the wisdom that succeeds anyhow," she cried, and she went on to tell the bitter results of the morning. "Oh, it is hard," she cried, "after all I have done, my friends won't be a whit better off!"

"It can't be lost," said the other. "You have saved him and he must——"

"*Must*," interrupted Gemma. "They say you cannot melt marble. I'd rather try to melt a man of marble than to get help from a devouring flame. *Must*—ah, you haven't seen him, haven't heard that voice. You might as well try to check the waves or silence the thunder. No, I am in despair—utter despair ! "

The listener watched her in silence.

" No Christian," she said at last, " can despair."

Gemma looked up quickly. " But what have I to hope ? For my country—slavery ; for myself—exile."

" No Christian is ever exiled," the Englishwoman said almost to herself.

" But you don't understand ! I am to leave Italy for ever, or for as long as Benito Mussolini is allowed to live. Ah ! why, why did I interfere to save him ? What an exquisite fool I have been."

"Dear Signora, it may have been folly, not wisdom, but don't get confused—all through your story it was quite clear that your folly was the folly of wishing to save an enemy. You find no reward from him, but you did not really do it to get his reward, that was a secondary motive. You did it from the folly of the Cross. Oh ! don't lose the infinite reward. Oh, don't be so deadly silly as to repent of what you did for God."

" Did I do it for God ? " Gemma looked puzzled for a moment, then like one waking from delirium—
" Yes, I did start doing it for God, I hope I went on doing it for God, but I am not sure—I don't know."

" But He knows."

They were silent for a full ten minutes with such a silence as seemed not only possible but easy at that place and time.

" But what shall I do now ? " burst from Gemma.

" I hope I did right, but see how I have failed. You English have been free too long, to love liberty as some of us do. It has been our passion. I thought if I saved his life he might let us be free, an honourable constitutional opposition ! He could do it if he chose ! "

" You worked for what seemed best, for an ideal state, and you were quite right. I know it is hardest of all to give up the noblest things. But we have to do that too at times in our lives."

" But when it's wrong to give up ? "

" But when you do more harm than good because you won't give up ? " The mystic's commonsense hurt Gemma.

" I don't suppose it much matters what I do now," she cried, " what I do or don't do any more." The first bell for vespers sounded harshly, the old nun rose to her full height. " It matters just as much as it ever mattered," she said.

" Which is not at all."

" What you do now as a Christian matters more than anything in creation that is not of the soul," said the old woman. " It matters infinitely just now what even an old woman like myself, whom nobody needs, does or does not do, because it matters to God."

That evening the Prioress took a turn in the garden

with the English sister, who was old in years but so young in the community that smiling young nuns looked up at the exquisite old face and called her " my child."

The Prioress was built on large lines, was sallow, with narrow shrewd eyes, and a full tolerant mouth. She and the Englishwoman felt a strong mutual attraction.

" How did the Duce treat her ? "

" Just what was to be expected. He clearly understood and trusted her, and she could do nothing with him, nothing at all ! She has told me a great deal about herself and I respect her immensely. I feel for her, for her love of liberty. You know, Mother, what partly drew me to our order is the spirit of individual liberty."

" But, Heavens ! " came in the deep voice of the other. " How does the Duce interfere with that ? There is so much confusion talked about liberty. I ask you if there are not more men and women free to live their own lives under a firm government than in utter chaos ? Peace, security, healthy conditions, work and rest—what do you want more ? You have all that in England no doubt, but, as I understand, you worry and fuss and wear yourselves out in public disputes and committees and votes and continual talk—talk—talk—no time to think, no time to pray, no leisure for home life. Now we are ready to leave all that bother to the Fascisti, and we find they do the tiresome things very well."

" But a tyrant grows heavier and heavier on the

back that bears him," said the old novice. " Half the horrors of history are under tyrants. Too much power corrupts."

" Have tyrants been the only corrupt rulers ? There is a corruption that comes from insecurity of power depending on pleasing the people."

The Englishwoman suppressed her answer, she did not want a mere argument, she wanted to get at the opinions of a woman whom she believed to be more spiritual even than she was shrewd. The silence was broken by the Superior, who perhaps herself felt the temptations of a ruler in her own little kingdom.

" I hope that his passion for work, the enormous amount of the difficulties of his job, may save him— he is not a military dictator, who, once arrived, can leave much to his generals. I will tell you how the Duce strikes me. He seems to me an instrument of God fashioned for our times, conscious of his own strength and of the weakness of other men ; he has the gift of absolute concentration on the work in hand. He is not troubled with the necessity for abstract thought, or with doubts, now that he has found his place in the world. Every now and then God sends, not a saint, not a superman, but just something strong enough, alive enough to control a country and raise it up. These tools for God's purpose may, while doing what they are made for, spoil and lose themselves. I know that even if he saves Italy he may lose his own soul. But, my child, there is a great cloud of prayer going up night and day in this land for the soul of Benito Mussolini."

THE SHADOW OF MUSSOLINI

The English novice had not, since the losses that had cut her life in two, been able to feel much interest in the drama of earthly life.

" We must go in," said the Italian.

" I shall be distracted at my prayers," said the widow almost as a joke.

The Superior spoke a little sternly. " My child, I want you to be of use to this soul, all the others are too Fascist in their feelings to be so. They would be kind, but you can give more sympathy. Only remember you can only help others if you do not neglect yourself. Your temptations in this house and garden, that looks so peaceful, may be quite as bad for the soul as the temptations of the Duce are for his. All in a convent seems small and childlike to those who don't know, but here the battle of good and evil is fierce and continuous. See what you can do without intrusion for this poor lady, you can even tell each other how you love liberty. Pray for her peace and my conversion."

" Yes, Mother," said the novice, who was quite accustomed to this request from the holy woman she loved with a friendship that was a deep joy in a life that had become lonely.

CHAPTER IV

A VISIT FROM THE DUCE

THERE were many penances offered habitually by the sisters of the convent for the Duce, a fact that would not have surprised him in the least, but there was one that cost them dear. It was of free will on the part of the Prioress and a willing submission on the part of the others. This was the decision of the Superior that the Duce should be seen and heard only by Gemma. For he was coming, and the warning of his coming was given only two hours before his motor was heard on the road. Nearly every sister owed him some personal debt of gratitude. Quite a number said that a father or a brother had come back to his religion since the putting down of the Freemasons—a few had known that the property of their families had been saved from destruction, others had gained from the mere possibility of a peaceful life—and as a community, that last was the amazing result of Fascism. The younger ones had had no hope of seeing their hero, but they had looked forward to the Prioress and the sub-Prioress, the second of whom was good at description, telling them all about him. The Prioress herself had quite a few minutes of eager expectation before she saw what she thought she must do and turned to the glowing sub-Prioress.

" The Duce will be in a hurry, he will ask for the Signora, who will be waiting in the large parlour outside the grille. He is coming to see her, not us, his time is precious. If he asks to see me, well and good, but if not——"

The sub-Prioress understood discipline as well as any Fascist officer. She winked away a bright little tear as she walked down the passage. It is to be hoped she will see the Duce in Heaven !

Gemma had steeled herself for another guarded journey to Milan, perhaps another police search of her person. She had not thought that Mussolini would come out to see her. The sub-Prioress brought her the news and then waited in silence, half wondering whether Gemma would wish to prepare herself in any way and would like help.

Gemma, at the moment, felt a tightening of the throat and then an idiotic inclination to laugh. She was startled and amazed at his coming. Since she had seen him she could take nothing about him or his doings lightly. Yet she felt a glimmer of amusement at the contrast between the nun's veneration and her own scorn, between the nun's idea of the man and her own.

The two lay sisters came to bring her out of the enclosed side of the convent to the part open to visitors. She asked them to let her wait in the chapel ; she would hear the motor. She heard it and went to receive him.

A VISIT FROM THE DUCE

The Duce came quickly into the bare parlour, with its forbidding grating across the end of the room.

She noticed that he looked old for his years, the hair about the square forehead was thin. He looked brighter than when in Milan, indeed he came in expecting to have a few genial words—he hoped they would be very few—with a Fascist Reverend Mother, and the beauty of the drive had been refreshing. He became grave, even solemn, at the sight of Gemma. and bowed with the look of immense respect he had shown when they parted at Milan.

"I came, Signora, to finish our conversation." They stood facing each other in the full light from the large windows.

"What is the use?" she asked. He did not remind her that she had said they must meet again.

"I must and will explain," he said. "There were conditions on which the police insisted, offered by me and accepted by you—those have been fulfilled, all but one—namely, that after seeing me you would consent to go to England."

Gemma looked at him as few ever dared to look, and to her own relief she did not flinch.

"I consented to exile."

"You did not believe that that condition would be insisted upon."

"It seemed impossible."

"And I must keep you to your word and that for your own sake, for you are not safe in this country. Our Fascist discipline is magnificent, but in all times of crisis lunatics and semi-lunatics grow dangerous.

239

It has got about that the police believe that you
meant to kill me. I cannot answer for your life."

" I can take the risk," cried Gemma scornfully.

" I refuse to allow it," was the answer. " What
you have in your own choice is whether to go to
England or America, on an English or an American
ship."

" And how soon ? "

" Immediately after the Conference, wherever it is
held."

" A few, a very few weeks and then exile."

" To save your life."

" What is my life worth now ? "

" You cannot ask that," he answered, " with your
beliefs, your hopes, your charity—how can you ?
I have my work, my hand on the plough, but if I
had your faith in all that this convent means, all
that you, Signora, have chosen as your part in this
mad world ! You have still more reason for believing in the value of life. You have a Christian
apostolate."

She was silent from surprise.

" Ah ! " he went on, talking very quickly, " if your
party had left politics alone, if they had gone out
like the early Christians or the first Franciscans and
produced a great religious revival, what could I not
have done with them ? The devil is clever, he
wrapped up their minds in the superstitions of the
nineteenth century, in cobwebs from dusty old
Liberalism, so that they could not see what was
before them—votings, committees, decentralisation,

old quack discarded remedies when it was a time of life or death for Italy."

"And who," cried Gemma, flaming at the man they called ' The Flame,' " who began your work, who gave you the ideals you have borrowed and traded on ? "

" What ideals ? "

" The ideals of self-sacrifice, of work for the people, of the true *Risorgimento*."

" Who gave them to you and to me ? " he answered. " Can you claim a monopoly of Christian ideals ? Would you wish to ? Many will blame me as a hypocrite if I become in my outlook more and more Christian, if I recognise more and more the awful need for an unchanging authority in human affairs. To live is to change, but Heaven knows how much more time I may be given ! If my allotted span holds four years more it should be enough to finish my work and to leave the rest to my friends."

He had again forgotten that she, to whom he spoke, was not numbered among his friends, and his personal allusions were to her intolerable. He expected a retort, but Gemma, it seemed, had fallen silent, had perhaps hardly listened to his last words. In truth she had felt while he spoke as if any power, any force of resistance, had weakened. It was no use to have the last word, it was no use to cry out again that Christ had made men free. She had no more stones to throw at this giant.

The silence grew into something positive that wrapped them round.

Q

THE SHADOW OF MUSSOLINI

During the silence, Gemma's eyes being cast down for the first time, the Duce ventured on a long, long but reverent look as she stood before him in the strong light of the uncurtained window. Though not perhaps an abstract thinker, he had always been an artist in life, and what he saw now seemed to him to belong to those imponderable things that are of supreme importance. He was not thinking of her words, though some day they might come back upon him, but he was thinking that he had never seen before such a great woman, great in mind and in soul, most wonderfully great in the unconscious manifestation of both. He hoped never to forget the inspiration of her look, her bearing, even the lightly-folded hands, which far from being raised in any attitude of supplication lay white and still against the plain black skirt. The Duce hoped he should not forget, but life he knew to be packed with impressions through which a man of action must force his way without pausing and without looking back. He admired her, but he did not pity, he had no pity for the noblest things. He believed in Life, and he had only pity, if indeed he had pity at all, for the incurably weak. He had simply looked at her then with this intention of recording so great a human soul, not without some consciousness of his own contact with her. Perhaps he was pleased that the immense power he wielded over all men and women in his own world was not without its effect on Gemma.

At a long last she raised a thin hand vaguely in the air. It seemed to the watcher to be a gesture of dismissal and as such he accepted it. He was accustomed to honouring those who were above him when there were any so to honour, and nothing could have exceeded the reverence with which he bowed to the woman who had saved his life, and to whom he felt bound to refuse all return for that great gift. He had not even the wish to say, " Half of my kingdom is thine," for the very core of his creed was that she and he were of no consequence whatever in comparison to the good of that kingdom. He sent her into exile thinking that she was not indispensable, whereas Italy was in her debt for the only life that was indispensable, namely, his own.

As he came out of the convent the nuns were forgotten, the salute of the Fascist guard was not returned, and the Duce was quite half way to Milan before he began to dictate, to the secretary at his side, a letter on the sanitation of a village near Naples.

CHAPTER V

AN ILL WIND

THE devil has one advantage in Italy which is unknown in England. Italians have stronger nerves than we have, while ours are of a tougher description than those of the Americans. What is meant by nerves and all their delicate connections is not going to be discussed here, but whatever they are, the Italians only become really aware of the torments they can inflict when a sirocco wind is blowing. Then a gentle and calm nun will look at moments like a fairy-tale hag with a black cat sitting on her shoulder, and you have to look closely before discovering any signs of the fine struggle that her soul is putting up against the enemy that rides on the evil wind. Custom only makes the effects more cruel.

Gemma, born and bred in Florence, was peculiarly susceptible to the influence of the sirocco, whereas the English novice in her second year in Italy has not yet felt any of its horrors, and indeed thought it rather refreshing than otherwise. She had not been many months in the convent before she had learnt to recognise the symptoms that denoted a bad wind even before she was aware that it was blowing. At such times it was best to put off any difficult question that she would otherwise have carried to the Superior.

AN ILL WIND

The day might be bright, the country beautiful to gaze upon, but every member of the community looked to the Englishwoman as if they were pulling hard on all their spiritual resources to be able to bear life at all placidly.

" The Duce was with her a long time ? " said the Superior with a note of interrogation in the quiet tone of her voice.

" And Gemma herself," replied the novice, " had thought he had been with her for about a quarter of an hour."

" You must not break any confidence that the poor thing has put in you," said the Reverend Mother, " but if there is anything you can tell me that was not said in confidence, it would of course interest me very much."

" I cannot say that there was anything private to myself in what she said," the widow novice went on. " She hardly seemed conscious to whom she spoke. She did not seem exactly angry. I think she was prepared to find him as implacable as in their first talk. He will not let her stay in Italy."

The Superior gave a deep sigh. " What sadness there is in these days, far greater sadness than in my youth ! "

" He will not let her stay," the Englishwoman went on, " because he says that here and now her life would be in extreme danger. That fear she declares to be pure nonsense, but he said that the responsibility was his and not hers.

The Superior looked at the walls that had shut her in for so many years. What could she know of the dangers beyond them ?

" I suppose he knows," she said, " but it sounds to me a little melodramatic. However, she is safe here, and we will keep her " (there was a regal touch in the Superior's tone) " as long as she likes. The Duce would never drag her out of the convent. Did she give you any idea of when he thinks she must go into exile ? "

" No, that was so strange," was the answer. " She talked about the Duce, talked about Italy, and then, Mother, she began to speak about her young husband, and when she spoke of him she wept ; but she wept gently. She said that to-day, for the first time for years, he was very vivid to her.

" ' After all,' she said, ' it cannot be very long before I am with him again with the old joy made new.' "

" Poor young widow, what you say is wonderful to me ! I thought that there was something fierce in her nature, that she would hold on to the Christian virtues with a strong will, but that she would have a hard fight and have to fight in the dark."

They were silent for a moment, and then the Italian turned again to what had passed between Gemma and the Duce. What had the Duce actually said ?

" She did not tell me much of what he had said. What amazed me was what she had ventured to say to him. She began first saying a little about his amazing career. The little journalist, she said, the blacksmith's son, the man who broke stones on the road, has taken Italy in his hand, as he would tell you himself, to cleanse, to mould, to inspire as he thinks fit. And, Mother, though she spoke in irony, even in her sarcasms I felt that she had reacted, that she had in some way, some strange mysterious way, come under the influence of the man. I think that she threw herself with her whole force against him, the Tyrant and the Dictator, the man who sent her into exile, but that in some strange way he has left her less his enemy, and he has left her without petty spite or the temptation to revenge. Somehow, Mother, they were fighting each other in the upper air. I can't say what I mean. But, I wonder, could he have quite escaped getting something from her ? "

She stopped and the old Superior looked up with eyes that were unusually bright at the thin, white face of the novice, who was so much older and more experienced than herself. But after a few minutes the dominant idea to wish to know all that she could learn about the Duce made her speak.

" Well, if you can't tell me what the Duce said to her, can you tell me what she said to the Duce ? "

" From first to last," said the other, " I mean during both talks, it appears that she said the most astounding things. She told him exactly what she thinks of him now. She owned to the good he had done as she saw it, but claimed that her own party were doing far better, far better because thay had higher aims."

"My dear," said the Prioress quietly, "that is really absurd. These good people did some excellent things, but they were really compromising with the spirit of disorder. Priests are too innocent when they mix in politics."

"I couldn't follow all that very well," said the novice. "I was too ignorant of the whole question. But what struck me most was the way she seems to have warned him as to the future. She told him that as a tyrant he would inevitably lose touch with the people, he would be surrounded by flatterers who would never let him hear the truth. Above all, his followers would persuade him that all who were not his blind henchmen were his enemies and the enemies of Italy. The flatterers, the slaves to his every mood, would appear to be his best friends, and they would be his worst enemies, and if they turn against him, she said, though I am not sure if she told him this, if the Fascisti turn against him, who can save him? Cæsar could not be protected from his friends."

"That is true," said the Reverend Mother, "but Cæsar wanted a crown, and the Duce only wants to serve."

"Then she told me she did not find it hard as a Christian to pray for him, that he may be saved from all the dangers she sees like a dark cloud over his head. 'All the nuns here pray for him, I know. Would you ask them to pray too that the sacrifices we Italians of the Popolari make for our country may be rewarded by our God.' Then, Mother, she said a word about herself. 'I realise now,' she said, 'I

who have had many ambitions from which my
countrywomen are generally free, although I have
taken my values wrongly, I do see now that there
is no reward worth having that ends with death.' "

Thus ended the novice's report, for neither woman
spoke again before the chapel bell called them away
from the garden.

Very early next morning, as the sisters passed
through the cloister on their way to the chanting of
Prime, the sirocco had reached the convent and
the devil was in the wind. Gemma moved uneasily
in her sleep.

CHAPTER VI

So Die His Enemies

FEW things have been more insisted upon in the training of the mystical life than the truth that the imagination is not the soul, that feeling is not the will, that spiritual joy is no indication of spiritual progress. This training stood the sisters of this particular convent in good stead during the days when the evil wind insinuated itself into every cell and not less into the cells of the brain than into the narrow rooms in which each sister lived so many hours alone with God. Afterwards thay had a special interpretation of the trouble of those days. They told themselves that the Prince of this world and the powers of darkness had been allowed to give a final test of a soul that should be without flaw, that should have known its purgatorial cleansing on this earth. At the time the Mother Prioress spoke to the English widow as to Gemma in her wise, unintrusive manner, " The poor lady," she said, " does not seem to be going to the chapel as she did."

" She has not been into the chapel for a day and and a half," was the reply.

" I wish she could find help and comfort."

" She was singularly comforted," answered the Englishwoman, " as it seemed to me, even after the talk with the Duce. She took things then in so large a fashion. There was nothing petty or revengeful."

" He makes life great," said the Prioress.

But it was not the Duce's greatness that interested the Englishwoman at that moment ; it was the fate of the woman whom, after all, for whatever motive, he was sending into exile. Exile was an unknown punishment to the Englishwoman. She had never known anybody exiled from her own country. It was an awful punishment, a punishment where a great reward was due.

" She was wonderful that evening," said the novice, " she was so calm and she talked with a strange weird eloquence."

" I often notice," said the Prioress, " that we Italians surprise you English by our manner of talk, but I honour this poor young widow that her manner of talk was not quite of another sort, a sort that might have surprised you in a very different way."

They were standing, the Prioress and the novice, in an alley of the garden, and at that moment their low voices fell away into silence, for at the cross alley, some ten yards from them, her head rising some way above the line of rose trees, gay in their mellow autumn bloom, came Gemma. They looked but a moment and then they turned away, not for fear that she should see them but from the instinctive dislike of intrusion, of moral impertinence. They looked at each other as they walked slowly up a little hill in silence, and then, as they turned into the convent, the old woman murmured, "*Il nostro, Signore, Gesù* allowed Himself to be in the power of the Devil that He might understand with human understanding the suffering of that poor soul."

Late that night the Prioress had shut the door of her cell, when there came a knock, and she opened the door to see the tall figure and transparent face of the English novice waiting for permission to speak. The Prioress gave her the usual signal and then a wonderful brightness, a smile that was extraordinarily young, lit up the face of the old woman. "La Poverella," said the English novice, "is kneeling in the chapel when she ought to have gone to her cell. Need I disturb her ? "

"Let her alone," said the Prioress, "she will soon go to rest. And, sister, I feel that she will sleep well."

Matins brought them all together, and when they came into the chapel they found Gemma still kneeling as the English novice had left her, but when they were all there and the office had begun, Gemma went away, went to her cell and slept very lightly. It seemed to her that the sweet northern air which now blew in at the window was like a little message from her Divine Lover, a little sign that He would give her joy of all kinds. It gave a sort of completeness to this rich sense of peace, such peace as she had never known before, a peace of a certain security of continuance that was without any tremulous uncertainty, any of the pathos of the foreknowledge of her own weakness in days to come. Daylight found her wide awake, still gloriously happy. She got up at the first sign of pink in the sky, washed and dressed herself with a certain reverent carefulness, whereas in the last two or three days she had been a little neglectful of a person that seemed of so little consequence. She passed out into the enclosed garden and walked down the little hill and turned to the left to look the better at the now dying glow of the sunrise which still washed with an exquisite pink the whole of the blue heaven. She came as far as the wall on the western side and leant her back against an old stone buttress. There, close to her hand, was one of those strangely beautiful autumn roses that hold the garnered sweetness of the summer. She had no wish to pick it, but she bent her head to drink in its sweetness and she murmured, " Jesus, I thank Thee for the beauty of this world." As she raised her head, she gave the opportunity that was needed. She never saw who fired the shot, possibly she never knew that man had killed her. As she thanked God for the beauty of this world, she came face to face with the beauty of its Maker.

The English novice went out into the garden to find Gemma, for she had missed her at Mass. It was about half-past six, when enjoying the lightness and brightness, the sense of the present peace and the aftermath of the joy of her thanksgiving, she too turned to the west. In a few moments she came beneath the old wall and saw what lay at the foot of the buttress. There was nothing at first sight to show what had been done to Gemma except the position in which she lay; the face was happy in death, perhaps even happier than when she left the chapel at the hour of Matins A big branch of the rose-tree had been broken by her fall, and the leaves of the rose she had not plucked were scattered and had fallen on the white forehead and the black hair. By her side there lay a little ball of crushed paper.

The Englishwoman had enough knowledge to see unmistakably that Gemma had indeed fallen asleep, had been in the phrase of the old martyrology this morning " born into a better life." After the novice had brought the Prioress to see Gemma, after they had with a number of the nuns carried her reverently into her little cell and knelt round her for a time in silence, the Prioress sent for the lay sisters who lived in the outer part of the convent, and they in their turn summoned the Fascist Guard. The Fascist officer was seen by the Prioress in the bare parlour where the Duce had talked to Gemma. She spoke from behind a grille and gave him what amounted to her orders as to what must pass in her own little kingdom. She wished him to send at once for the Duce and to bring out the Vicar-General from Milan. " You will tell no one else of this crime after you have told the Duce. Of course you will go first to him."

" But, Mother Prioress," interrupted the Fascist officer, " the Duce is in Rome."

" Well then," she answered, " you will of course communicate with him. Bring me without delay the

SO DIE HIS ENEMIES

Vicar-General by whose orders I admitted the
Signora to what I believed to be a place of
safety."

Fascist officers do not as a rule quail before any
human being except the Duce himself, but the officer
of the guard that had been placed at this convent
understood and received the rebuke with an overpowering sense of shame.

A bow of dismissal from the other side of the
grille which divided the parlour sent him away, and
the motor took him with extreme speed down into
Milan.

Two hours later the Prioress and the Vicar-General
—a tall thin man with stooping shoulders and very
white hair—were discussing the necessary decisions
to be come to, such as for permission to be given to
the police to enter the closed garden, and any other
details following upon this death within the precincts.
They were both profoundly agitated, but intimate
friends as they were, with long habits of mutual
advice given and taken on both sides, he knew that
while her sorrow and trouble was laid open to him,
she was all the time hiding something, and that
something he was determined to know.

" It's of no use, Mother Prioress," he said at last.
" You must tell me what it is."

" What it is ? " she faltered.

" Any woman can conceal anything from any
man," he said with a sad kind smile, " if she has really
determined to do so, but you, most reverend Prioress,

are undecided as to whether to conceal the truth or not."

"Take it then," she said, and threw a small ball of paper through the bars of the grille. It fell at his feet, and as he bent to pick it up she said, "It was found by the murdered body."

He opened the paper which bore the well-known Fascist design and the address of a club in Milan, and there was on it, written in Italian, very few words, "So die all the enemies of Mussolini."

BOOK VI

CHAPTER I

BEFORE PATSEY HEARD

FOR some weeks after leaving Italy life was much simplified for Patsey. Lady Lavington was too ill to travel, and in Geneva they must stay. Probably they would not move before Christmas. There was just a touch of anxiety conveyed by the admirable Swiss doctor in his expressions of reassurance. Although untrained, Patsey was not a bad nurse and she became absorbed in charts of temperature and food. She could refuse all invitations without giving offence, and she only saw the cousins occasionally. She was spared questions about Dick and his mother simply out of kindness. It was not from want of interest, but the gossip had been brought to a head when she came back with no sign of being engaged. Clearly the Florence expedition had been a failure. Some said that the great Mrs. Milward had not approved, and despised Dick's want of courage; others that Patsey had, to put it crudely, just tried and failed. Anyhow, there was clearly nothing doing. The coming meeting of the Foreign Ministers at Lausanne was the excitement. Patsey lay awake all one night after she was finally convinced that the Duce had after all ignored the great warning. She was overwhelmed with the disappointment. She had failed to find out anything about Gemma. She did not doubt that permission to see the Duce had been given, but it was impossible to discover if Gemma had gone to Italy or not. It was no use to go on like this trying to think of nothing but the routine of the sickroom. It was only a week from the date fixed for the Congress. Up to now she had fully expected to hear that another place had been chosen. This evening her cousin from the Secretariat had looked in to ask after Lady Lavington. She had suddenly, blushing hotly to his astonishment, asked the old man if he were sure that there was no change of plan. " None whatever ! Why should there be ? " He and his daughters were going to stay in Lausanne, as he must be at the station to meet the English Foreign Minister, and they wanted to see the arrival. Then, seeing Patsey's embarrassment, and dimly conscious that something was supposed to have gone wrong in the girl's life, he impulsively added, " Why not come too ? If Aunt Mary is better, a little change will do you good ? " The lovely face, as the kind man thought it, suddenly lost all its sadness. " Thank you, thank you."

It was the most astonishing relief, this idea of being on the scene of action after all—not being so horribly out of things. If the Duce *would* come, if no one would believe in the danger, she, Patsey, at least would see things to the bitter end. She suddenly looked up at the important person with an intense temptation to confide the whole thing to him, but she seemed to hear the Duce commanding her to be secret. " Poor child . . . stupid feller, Milward . . . dreadful old mother. . . ." Patsey's hand was shaken very warmly, and she was left in a very tempest of excitement. " Oh, if only Aunt Mary improved in the next few days ! "

But was there absolutely nothing to be done to prevent the awful danger hanging over Italy, over Europe ? Patsey as she lay awake felt the burden of her silence almost unbearable. For the only human being to whom she could say a word was Dick Milward, and he had shown no sign of life. Unlike the modern way and custom, he had taken a refusal as a dismissal from the presence of the lady. He did not play about lightly, while giving an occasional sigh or a bitter jibe at life. He was gone out of her life altogether, and she was left alone. And he had left her with the shaft of reproach—" You were very generous, Patsey, but were you quite just ? "

She did not even know where he was or where to address a letter to him. She supposed he had followed the Duce, but she could hardly send a letter " c/o Signor Mussolini." There was no one to whom to say, " Isn't this sheer madness ? Isn't it positively criminal to allow the Conference to be held at Lausanne ? "

As she tossed in that white night, during which her pillow seemed like that famous pillow of St. Francis to be possessed by the Devil, through all the long hours Patsey felt the growing need of Dick.

THE SHADOW OF MUSSOLINI

The day was bright when she fell asleep, a dreamy, uncomfortable sleep, and she woke up saying to herself, " Rodney Castle." She could not imagine why. "Rodney Castle—oh, no, no ! not Rodney Castle ! " She was sitting up, her face buried in her hands. She shivered when she said, " Oh, no." A new day in this wretched thing called life, in which one thing was clear : she had no use whatever for Rodney Castle.

Then looking again at the tray, she knew why she had said, " Rodney Castle," for there a letter from him was lying by the plate of rolls. She must have seen it before she was half awake. She opened it at once.

" DEAR PATSEY,

" Don't think me a bore if I ask for any news you can give me. I have been hearing so many rumours that I am anxious for facts. Last night I was in company, as they used to say, with two or three men, one of whom, a journalist, had just come from Milan. Goodness, how he loathes and abominates Mussolini. If he were a whit less violent his description of things would affect one a good deal. As it is, one wonders if so much smoke can come from nothing. He declares he knows an old man, a fine old Liberal of the Manzoni tradition, was beaten to death in a café by a number of young Fascists for merely criticising the present régime ! Also the castor oil has wrecked hundreds ! But what I want to ask you about is his story about

Gemma, for it surely must be Gemma ! He described a woman—a lady beautiful and intellectually distinguished, a Florentine, the widow of a poet—who got mixed up with the Socialists in Switzerland. It seems that she managed to get to Milan on the plea that she must see the Duce and warn him of his enemies. The Fascists were furious at his consenting to see her. But this journalist fellow actually says it was a trick of Mussolini's to get her and keep her, and that she is imprisoned in a convent. He alarmed me very much, for he added in a low voice, ' I should be very sorry to insure that beautiful woman's life.'

" I suppose that is sheer prejudice, but what is one to believe ? It drives me mad that I am worse than useless, for if I went to Italy, with the Fascist police knowing that I took her to Switzerland, I could only do harm."

Patsey gasped with excitment and let her coffee grow cold. Then Gemma had got to Milan—had surely seen the Duce. The rest, of course, was sheer nonsense. There was a fresh date on the second sheet of notepaper two days later than the first.

" I am glad," Rodney went on, " that I did not post this before, because I have now much more valuable information from a man whom you know, Dick Milward. He was at Balliol and was dining there last night. I had some words with him, and then he came back to New College with me and we talked late into the night.

263

"I am not sure I should have put that *more* valuable information came from him, as he did not know the story from Milan, but he has quite convinced me that the journalist, whom he knew in Italy, is utterly unreliable. He only hopes that Gemma did get to Milan, for there she would be safe from all danger. She was in great danger in Switzerland from the scoundrels who were trying to make use of her. He has brought me back to the view of the Duce that even Gemma did not destroy for me. The man, whatever his faults, is strangely, curiously right in his ideal and his appeal. Milward has told me of his plans for the solution of the labour troubles, of his insistence on obedience and sacrifice in all classes alike. I am hardly inclined to idealise the Popolari since they threw over Gemma. I heard the other day that her brother has gone as a missionary to Africa, leaving all politics, to preach the Gospel.

"I like Mr. Milward immensely ; he has remarkable powers. I don't think the Duce has treated him well, for I felt a certain generosity in his tone. Unconsciously he was more generous than grateful, it seemed to me. He asked me if you ever wrote to me, and I said you used to write fairly often, but not since you had gone to Florence. He said, ' If you write to her tell her from me that I have enjoyed a talk with you without betraying one of the Duce's secrets or anybody else's.' I ventured one query before he left me at two in the morning, because I could not help it : ' Will the Conference, after all that has been done and suffered, be held at Lausanne ? '

" He said, ' Yes. I heard this morning at the Foreign Office that the Marquis has taken his rooms there.'

" Then I saw how much he felt the terrible sense of a dark fate not to be put off. ' The Ides of November have nearly come,' he said, and went away in silence.

" But, Patsey, that Gemma is safe is the one thought in my heart. And Patsey, having said so much, I must add this : I have not the least hope of my ideal being realised, but I have got it with me for always. With it I can never, I hope, be merely the man I was. By it I test all intellectual sincerity, all camouflaged ambitions, all the mere warmth of social vanity. Probably she has forgotten me.

" Forgive so long a letter. I send it all, for the second sheet will at once relieve the anxiety you will feel only for a moment.

" Ever yours,
" RODNEY CASTLE."

Patsey drank her cold coffee mechanically—her thoughts in Rodney's rooms at New College, where she and Aunt Mary had lunched only a year ago. And Rodney liked Dick immensely ! And Rodney had all he meant to want, and Dick had nothing but disappointment as far as she knew.

Rodney had recognised that Dick was generous ;

she liked to think of those two together. She glowed at the thought that Gemma had really and truly seen the Duce, and then, in the midst of all this almost unbearable excitement, she remembered that in a week's time Mussolini would drive through the streets of Lausanne. It was like a great gloom of stormy darkness against which there were glimmers of brightness. If only Dick, who knew it all, would come and stand with her in the Lausanne station. Then she hurried to be ready for the Swiss doctor, who expressed the utmost confidence that Patsey would be able to leave her aunt, without any fears and scruples, for the visit to Lausanne.

" You will see M. Poincaré," he said kindly, " and the Signor Mussolini ! "

" Yes," sighed Patsey, " I shall see the Signor Mussolini ! "

CHAPTER II

AFTER PATSEY HEARD

PATSEY spent an exceedingly quiet day. There was
no immediate anxiety for Lady Lavington, and she
followed the doctor's advice in not giving too much
thought to the morrow; and the atmosphere of the
sickroom, with its flowers and its midday sunshine
and its amusing fiction, produced a cheerfulness
which was not merely assumed by the aunt and the
niece. But in the back of Patsey's mind there were
a picture and a problem, the picture was of Dick
Milward talking with Rodney Castle. The thought
of these two together for the first time gave her
furiously to think. The picture became so living she
could not have put it into words, but she did wonder
with amazement at herself that she could ever have
been interested in what seemed now a shadowy,
almost a dull—there was no shirking the word—a
dull friend. He still had a certain charm of a dull
kind, she still had a sympathy with him in his
curious, rather pale romance, the romance of one
figure in the stained glass of a lancet window for
another figure in another lancet window. She liked
him now in his almost superstitious anxiety for
Gemma—for Gemma who was not dull at all.

Gemma in Milan! For clearly she had got to

Milan, and the Duce would take good care of her. She tried to picture to herself the meeting between the man from whose flame had been detached just a little flame that would never be extinct in her own imagination, or perhaps what Patsey thought or called her imagination, in this case her heart. How had the Duce taken Gemma's warning? It would seem not at all, for that wretched Conference was to be held in Lausanne after all. It was too incredible! She knew—for had she not seen Mussolini—that he was an absolute necessity, now at least, for his country's welfare. It might be true, though it was hard to believe it, but in four years' time, if one of the pack of wolves that are after him brought him down, he would leave a country not only purified, not only holding a great seat in the councils of the world, but capable of unity in rule, in religion, in vigour, and in happiness, capable of having and of being all these things without Benito Mussolini. And she had known, too, that he had been perfectly aware that it would be treason to his own country to expose his life before his work was done ; possibly she excited herself with these thoughts about the Duce, pictured to herself rather wilfully those over-powering eyes that had looked at her with so much candour and so much racial reserve.

Tea, the pale China tea to which we have grown accustomed, had given its slight fillip to their cheerfulness, and Patsey had taken up the local evening paper and was unfolding its damp, small sheets, when a servant coming in told Lady Lavington that

AFTER PATSEY HEARD

Monsieur Milward was below asking to see *ces dames*. A bright flush came into Lady Lavington's white cheeks at this announcement, but Patsey's colour did not change.

"What shall we do, my dear?" said the lady who had been bred under Queen Victoria.

Patsey, turning to the servant, said that she would descend immediately. She then proceeded to do what is called making the invalid comfortable, though the invalid, if she happens to be comfortable already, probably does not gain by the process. While her pillows were being put where she did not want them to be, and her hot-water bottle was forced on her warm and reluctant feet, and the novel she had finished was put within her reach, Lady Lavington avoided Patsey's glance, and murmured nothing but "Thank you, my dear. That's all right." She had not even the courage to ask for the evening paper which now lay on the floor. Presently Patsey stalked out of the room, her back conveying a certain sense of displeasure to the now feverish Lady Lavington.

Downstairs Patsey looked into the big lounge, and seeing no Dick Milward, but only groups of other people drinking their tea, turned into the small salon where visitors who had sent up their names were often kept waiting. She had thought it would be quite easy to meet Dick without any silly, old-fashioned embarrassment, and she had even at the moment forgotten the sense of guilt towards him which she had often remembered with real pain ever since they had parted.

She had expected a cheerful, unembarrassed Dick who had recovered from his mood in Florence, and as she had come downstairs rather slowly she had told herself that she did not and would not mind in the very least. What she was not prepared for was what she found. Dick Milward stood on the other side of a round table, both hands it seemed almost holding on to the mahogany, and he did not leave go of this support, nor did he even bow, even when she came forward and stood smiling at him with only the small table between them.

"Patsey," he stammered, "have you seen the evening paper?"

She was so astonished that she actually said "Yes," without adding that though she had held it in her hand she had not read one line of it.

He looked at her in amazement, and she began to notice that he was not only pale and nervous but untidy, and even, although it seemed incredible in Dick Milward, he looked as if he had neither shaved nor washed. Patsey began to be frightened.

"Something has happened?" she cried.

"Yes," he answered. "Something terrible has happened, and I have come straight through from London because I did not want you to be without anybody who would understand if you were upset."

"Dick," she said, "for heaven's sake don't go on breaking the thing. I am prepared now for any news. Have they shot the Duce?"

He sat down suddenly, and leaning on the table covered his face with his hands. Patsey came round the table and put her hand on his shoulder. " What is it, Dick ? Can it be Gemma ? "

Dick groaned. " Yes, Patsey, they have shot Gemma. And, Patsey, it's the Fascisti who have shot Gemma. They are saying in London and in Paris that this is a fresh instance of what befalls the enemies of Mussolini."

Patsey sat down on the chair next to Dick's. " Where did this news come from ? " she said sharply. " There are so many lies. Are you sure she's dead ? Are you sure any of it is true ? "

" No one has denied it, no telegram contradicting it has come through from Milan. It appeared first in the *Evening Standard* as a Paris telegram. I might have missed it, only that Rodney Castle rang me up from Oxford."

Patsey's expression had had its usual look of readiness for whatever might come, and the certain determination not to mistake good for evil, not to look on the black side of things, and, above all, not to quail before the possibly hard blows of Fate. It is only the very sensitive, who have imagination and who know the need of self-mastery, who have quite that look. Now for the first time, Dick saw Patsey give way to a sense of utter defeat, or rather he saw her overwhelmed beyond any power of holding out. She did not cry, she did not look at him for sympathy, she seemed rather to be gazing at some object in the dark shadowed corner of the waiting-room. " It was I," she said, not to him, " it was I who sent Gemma to her death."

Dick was frightened. He put his hand on her arm and he felt it to be rigid.

" It was I," Patsey went on, " who sent her into that trap."

" No, Patsey, no," said Dick.

" But I did," said Patsey, still without looking round. " I did wrong. I behaved so abominably to you. I would meddle. Oh, my God, here is my punishment."

" But Patsey, dear Patsey, anyone in their senses would have supposed that she was far safer in Italy than in Switzerland."

" What do they say ? " demanded Patsey. " How did she die ? Where did she die ? "

" She had been shut up in a convent," said Dick, " guarded by Fascisti. She tried to escape, and they shot her. She was found dead in the garden."

" But that isn't true, you know," said Patsey. " It can't be true just like that. Yet they couldn't say that she was dead if she were not dead, and "— and then she wailed again, " it's my fault, Dick, it's no use contradicting me, it's my fault that she is dead. In the name of heaven, why couldn't I have left things alone ? Why don't we trust Providence more, Dick ? Oh, I don't know," then, turning to him, " Oh, Dick, it was good of you to come to me. It was splendid of you."

Patsey was past being observant or she might have seen that praise from her was just what Dick Milward found it very hard to bear, but he did not think of himself for more than a moment, and to overcome the sense of his own hurt he put his arm round her, and said, in a low and very gentle voice, very unlike his usual tone in speaking even to her :

" Look here, Patsey, you must not be ill. You must trust God in a real big way. You meant no harm. Nobody in their senses could have done anything better than you did as far as you had ground to go upon. You were perfectly right to trust the Duce."

" To trust the Duce ? " cried Patsey.

" You don't mean," said the astonished Dick, " that you think the Duce has had anything to do with Gemma's death ? "

" I don't really, Dick. It makes me sick. I don't, indeed I don't ; but it's like a nightmare. I'm all confused. It seemed to me that that newspaper was telling lies, but when you said, as if you believed it, how she had been killed and where she had been killed, I felt—Oh, I know I'm an idiot—I felt as if I'd been one among the crowds and crowds of people that had fallen under his influence, but that in my heart I believed him capable even of this."

" My dear Patsey," said Dick, " that is just because you have had a shock. Believe me, it's all nonsense. For one thing, what on earth could the Duce gain but utter mistrust, general discredit for such a crime ? I know him very well, very well, Patsey, and I have myself suffered from his faults. But if there is one thing of which he is proud beyond another, it is that the Fascist revolution has been singularly free from the stain of bloodshed. Why, his worst enemy could

s

not have done him more harm than this murder.
But I have thought lately that he has been more
easily deceived. If there are men who are crazy
against him in Italy, there are still more men, and
a very large number of women, who are crazy in their
worship of him. I have found his psychology singularly true and his sense of character ; witness how
he believed in you at first sight and how he took
your account of Gemma. Believe me, none of that
was play-acting. But the atmosphere, something
like the atmosphere of a religious revival of which
he is the hero, is bad for any man's powers of dis-
crimination. All of which simply means that the
blackshirt may conceal from the Duce the black
heart inside it. I know myself that he does not spare
punishment when he discovers villainy. There are
in the prisons many more Fascists than his enemies
choose to believe."

Patsey, very white and very still, was drinking in
all that he said to her with an immense sense of
restored faith. He got up suddenly and opened a
window, letting in the air of the glorious autumn
evening into the stale-smelling little waiting-room.
Then again putting his arm round her, he turned her
face towards the fresh air.

" You look better now, Patsey," he said.

" But," she answered in a stronger voice, " even
apart from that mad idea as to the Duce, which
hurts me horribly like a nightmare, don't you see,
Dick, that if she had stayed in Switzerland she
could not have been shot. She would be alive

now, and I—I should not have this horror." She shuddered.

Dick looked out and caught a faint glimpse of the evening star rising above the dark trees in the garden, before he answered her.

" Patsey, there were plenty of Communists in Switzerland who might have shot her. You got her out of the infernal regions, for she could not have left this country or got back into Italy if she had been left to herself. And don't you think, Patsey, that the Gemma of whom you have told me was one of those people who are marked out for tragedy, one of those people who make even an ordinary fellow like myself feel that there must be another world, just because they are so unsuited to this one."

Patsey had hardly seemed to know that the strong arm was holding her towards the air. She had not looked up at him, but now he said :

" Tell me, Patsey, don't you think that's true ? "

" Yes, Dick, I think it is extraordinarily true."

Then suddenly she looked into his face.

" Patsey," he said, " I've a sort of an idea that something else is true."

" Yes," said Patsey, " it's quite, quite true, Dick," and she laid her head very quietly to rest on the rough coat still covered with the dust of his journey.

It was so inevitable, so a matter of course that they should belong to each other, that they felt that their past lives too had been led together. It was as

THE SHADOW OF MUSSOLINI

if two young children had for a long walk held each
other's hands and would go up the hill all the rest
of the way together, and together would come down
the inevitable descent on the way home.

CHAPTER III

PREPARING FOR THE CONFERENCE

MANY holy folk, many good folk, make sacrifices to give pleasure to others, which too often fail of their effect; but one thing that never fails of its effect in causing joy is a happy engagement. All the bells began to ring, so to speak, in the little international world of Geneva in the autumn. One special note rang from the heart of Lady Lavington, a very clear, very sweet note, for nothing pleases the old so much as to see a happy start in life—life, which cannot give much more to themselves. It really made Aunt Mary positively well, and her bedroom, which fortunately was large, was often nearly full with those who came to rejoice with her.

There was a little sting, of course, hints that after all Patsey's journey to Florence had not been in vain, hints that Patsey was a clever girl who knew how to be rich as well as happy, hints that Mrs. Milward might have looked higher, that, in fact, part of Patsey's glory lay in the fact that Dick Milward might have married almost anybody. But these incidental thorns in conversation were really buried in roses, and such little shafts quite annoy the kind hearts, that loose them almost unconsciously. The fact was, that everybody was so happy because they were lighting their fires at the bright and glorious warmth of the young lovers. It helped—this glow—to light up the sad, joyless ways in which most of the world were living. Faith was what they wanted, and faith in love, though it be only a mood, is better than no faith at all for a time.

> "They lit their lamps gone out
> At newer children's eyes."

But if their joy was so radiant as to be quite unmistakable any close observer might have noticed that they had their hours of anxiety—they were by no means free of care. Each day brought them nearer to the Lausanne Conference, and the men who were occupied with preparations for the said Conference would have been entirely surprised at the conversation of the two young people they had congratulated so warmly. Every time Dick and Patsey found themselves alone, two topics distracted them from the main and absorbing topic of themselves. The first was Mussolini. The second was Gemma and their astonishment at the silence of the press regarding her after the first insinuations.

"No news?" Patsey would ask, and Dick would shake his head.

"Surely there must be a trial. Nobody suspected even?"

"I should think dozens and dozens are suspected," said Dick, "and endless people preparing for the trial, but you can't get out of your British little head that if a thing is done, it is also done in print."

" Well," said Patsey, "it's a good thing the Italians have strong nerves. It would get on my nerves, I can tell you, to have to live in the dark."

" It gets far more on people's nerves in England that they are fed with every detail of murders and divorces and everything horrible. The Italians are remarkably happy at this moment. That is more than can be said of any other country I know. They are busy with their own concerns, and they are proud of their Mussolini to a comic degree. A witty Italian lady said to me in Rome : ' They love him so that if he asked them to cut off their noses they would rub those features with a gentle smile, and wonder if it were not possible to do without them.' "

" I wonder they let him come out of Italy at all," said Patsey.

" Let him ? " said Dick. " They know whatever they do, he will jolly well settle his movements for himself."

" Lausanne," said Patsey sadly. " Doesn't it drive you mad, Dick, to hear the people hear talking about Poincaré and the Marquis and the arrangements made for them in the hotel at Lausanne, and then alluding to the Duce as if he were of half their consequence ? Lausanne ! And Gemma died to prevent his going to Lausanne ! "

" I own," said Dick, " that I think it would be only decent if the Duce had taken her warning. He could surely have insisted on the Conference being held elsewhere. After all, it's only a few talks between three men that all this fuss is about."

"You will be at the station, Dick, won't you?" said Patsey. "I have been promised, solemnly promised, that I shall see everything that can be seen on the platform. The St. Gothard train will draw up on one side a few minutes before the train from Paris on the other, so one ought to see the Duce as he arrives first."

Dick had controlled himself as long as Patsey ran on, but now he turned upon her.

"The station at Lausanne," he cried. "I could not hear of such a thing. If it's dangerous for the Duce, good heavens! isn't it dangerous for you?"

Patsey was furious.

"My dear," she said in her most superior manner, "no one ever supposed for a moment that the Duce would be blown up or shot at inside the station. Why, my friends would think me crazy if I said I would not go with them to see the Ministers arrive."

And so there followed a quarrel, quite a sharp quick quarrel, a short quarrel because Patsey seized the moment when she could appear to climb down by agreeing to certain conditions, of which the chief was that she would leave the station by train and not come out into the streets in the wake of the Foreign Ministers.

She agreed to go out and dine with Dick at an admirable hotel at Ouchy. After dinner they would motor back to Geneva, "by which time," said Dick with a sigh, "whatever is to happen, will have happened."

That was only two days before the Lausanne Conference.

Time passed quickly in the next forty-eight hours, and Patsey's mind was so entirely full of what would happen next day that when Dick appeared suddenly in the dining-room she read the solemn, serene, eager look on his face, and she said to herself as he wended his way through the tables, "I am sure he has heard that the Duce is not coming," but he bent over her, and said very quickly in a low voice:

"They have got the murderers. One is a Russian, another Italian. They were caught at the frontier trying to get into Switzerland dressed as Fascisti. The Italian was recognised by the Swiss police as an anarchist only lately come back from Russia. 'Kill or be killed' is the motto of the Bolsheviks. Gemma was bidden to kill the Duce and instead she warned him. To the enemies of our civilisation that was intolerable. If Gemma could not be made a tool she must be made an object lesson—to those who will understand."

Patsey was looking very white. "I think *I* am beginning to understand," she said slowly. She left the rest of her dinner untasted, and they sat together in the lounge, devouring the news in the Swiss evening paper.

"Now," cried Patsey, "the English papers will have to apologise."

"Not they," said Dick. "In obscure corners you

will find telegrams from Berne, mentioning casually that two anarchists have been arrested, who are accused of having murdered this unfortunate lady, disguised as Fascists. And again and again, after about six months, they will allude to the treatment meted out to women who are anti-Fascists, and they will give us an instance in the vaguest terms of the well-known case of the lady who was supposed to have been murdered by Communists."

" Whatever happens," sighed Patsey, " Gemma is dead, and will not come to life again."

" Probably she would much rather not, if that's any comfort to you, Patsey."

CHAPTER IV

The Great Man's Gesture

THE station seemed to Patsey to be vastly big in its emptiness. There was no crowd to hide the length and breadth of the platform, and only two deserted trains could be seen in the far distance. The little English party, who were admitted only on delivery of orders signed by the head of the police, consisted of eleven. There was Aunt Mary's important cousin and his two daughters and Patsey and Dick Maitland. There was the First Secretary from Berne and the English Consul, and the journalist in high repute, with his photographer.

Patsey's cousins thought it extremely amusing to have the great empty station to themselves, but even they spoke in subdued tones of hilarity.

" I ask you," one sister said to the other, " if you ever in all your days saw anything to match the solemnity of Patsey's countenance."

" She and Dick," giggled the other in a suppressed murmur, " look as if they had come to meet a corpse. I never saw anything so funereal."

Meanwhile the important cousin had gained certain facts from the Chef de Gare. The special train bringing Signor Mussolini was expected to be before the train from Paris by as much as twenty minutes.

THE SHADOW OF MUSSOLINI

Monsieur Poincaré and the Marquis would come in the same train, each having a magnificent saloon, it appeared, and several carriages for both suites.

The Chef de Gare then, after many excuses, left the English party and went to welcome the half-dozen French officials who had been allowed to pass into the station. The French Minister from Berne was a magnificent-looking man who appeared to relish the fact that he was taller than any of the English party except perhaps Dick Milward. He was very kind to the English Secretary from Berne as the latter made his excuses for his chief, who was ill.

The two little parties mingled and various introductions were made to the English young ladies.

" What a fuss the police seem to be in. The streets are full of them," cried one of the cousins to an attractive young Frenchman.

" But, Mademoiselle, they have to convince three countries that they are doing their best."

" Curious," said the old French Consul at the same moment to his English colleague, " that the inn-keeper's son, who knew what it was to be very hungry in the streets of Lausanne, is one of the great ones of the earth for whom we are waiting."

" He is due now," said the Englishman, " and by the way, where is the Italian Consul ? "

The Chef de Gare now observed to the group near him that Signor Mussolini's train was late.

A little longer and then another railway official came up and greeted his chief.

" The Italian special has reached Territet," he said.

THE GREAT MAN'S GESTURE

" Then you gentlemen," said the Chef de Gare, " may expect Signor Mussolini in——"

It was now the turn of the member of the Secretariat from Geneva to wonder why no Italians had appeared to welcome the Duce. Dick drew Patsey a few feet away.

" What the dickens does it mean ? " he asked her. " The Italian Consul here is a sound Fascist and so, I happen to know, are the Italian diplomats at Berne."

" Do you think," murmured Patsey, " that he wants to go through it alone ? Isn't it amazing, Dick, to see all these people so smug and happy when they have been warned and warned and warned ? "

The Chef de Gare now asked the leading members of the English and French groups if they would come across the station to the far platform to welcome the Italian statesman.

" But have we time ? " cried the French Minister. " I must be at the door of Monsieur Poincaré's saloon the moment he arrives."

Nor would the representative of the English Legation and the Secretariat at Geneva risk not being on the spot when their Marquis should alight.

" Well," said the Chef de Gare, " I know not how to divide myself, and I'm not at all sure that we shan't have the Paris train first after all. There has been no signal to show that the train has left Territet."

The English and French groups now moved to where the Paris special would draw up and, knowing that Monsieur Poincaré would be in the front of the train, and the English Marquis in the second saloon, arranged themselves accordingly.

" I hope the Marquis will be satisfied with us," murmured one of the cousins to the other. " The French have got their Minister and the head of their Secretariat, and we have only the second fiddles in both. Still dear papa has beautiful manners, and we'll give him as graceful a reception as anybody."

The French special was now signalled, and then it came hustling and bustling with an extreme air of importance into the empty station.

The distracted Chef de Gare, who had received no signal from Territet, now hurried up to add to the welcome. He opened the door, hat in hand, for Monsieur Poincaré, who immediately came out attended by two Secretaries, and almost fell into the arms of the French Minister from Berne. The English Secretary, meanwhile, had opened the door of the Marquis's carriage. It was disappointing that no Marquis emerged, but Patsey's cousins were gratified at finding that their father was invited to enter and join the great man. They looked up to see the meeting through the windows of the carriage, but the blinds were drawn.

After the first greetings the French group seemed to be urging the stationmaster to produce Signor Mussolini, and Patsey heard him answer, " I will telephone to Territet instantly and find out what has caused the delay."

Monsieur Poincaré, arm in arm with the French Minister, walked quickly up and down the platform with some air of impatience. The stationmaster, who had hurried across to the telephone, now reappeared with two telegrams on a salver, one of which he offered to Monsieur Poincaré himself and the other was handed to the invisible Marquis.

Patsey and Dick, oblivious of all spectators, stood hand in hand and seemed incapable of answering any of the questions that everybody was murmuring to everybody else. The girls knew that they must not approach their father when he jumped down from the train and walked towards Monsieur Poincaré. Then to the general surprise, Monsieur Poincaré slowly mounted into his own saloon carriage followed by the French Minister and the Chef de Gare. It seemed to Patsey only a moment before the Chef de Gare reappeared, stood back a few feet from the carriages, gave a whistle and then a second whistle, the engine snorted and the special train from Paris moved off.

The English group remained complete. The representative of the Secretariat had gone no further. He turned to the diplomatist who stood nearest to him and spluttered out, "It's damned cheek! That Italian parvenu has made them go on to Territet. The Marquis said that we were not to make a fuss about nothing. Territet was merely a step from Lausanne. If Monsieur Poincaré was ready to go that step further, so was he. He left the decision to him, and Poincaré gave the orders to the stationmaster, but for polite cursing, I imagine what was going on in that train might make a navvy's hair stand on end."

He ruffled his hair with one hand as he spoke.

THE SHADOW OF MUSSOLINI

" Signor Mussolini has secured rooms, so kind of him, in the same hotel as his own and he will be at their disposal until to-morrow, when he must return to Italy for the funeral of a friend. It is the hugest bit of swagger I have ever heard of."

" And that," exclaimed the diplomatist, " from an Italian to Poincaré and our Marquis. It's an astounding gesture, and of course it would have been more ridiculous if the great men had remained in Lausanne while Mussolini remained in Territet. Now, the less said the better ! "

" I did hear," said the other, " the story that Mussolini had objected to Lausanne as a place where the atmosphere would be strongly biassed. I simply didn't believe it ! "

Patsey and Dick, as soon as the news was known, walked far away from the astounded mingled group of English and French. They could not speak for some moments and then, at a safe distance from the rest of the world, behind a deserted bookstall, he put his arm round her and murmured, " This is your doing, Patsey. It is you who saved him."

" Oh, no," cried Patsey. " Gemma saved him. I was only a messenger. Dick," she stammered, " Dick," and tears ran down her cheeks, " Dick, did you hear that in the telegram the Duce said he must go back to-morrow for a funeral. Do you think it's possible "—she broke down—" that he has gone to Gemma's funeral ? "

" Yes, Patsey, I do."

www.ingramcontent.com/pod-product-compliance
Lightning Source LLC
Chambersburg PA
CBHW031002260626
47169CB00002B/653